RUN
AND GUN

Eric Howling

James Lorimer & Company Ltd., Publishers
Toronto

James Lorimer & Company Ltd., Publishers acknowledges funding support from the Ontario Arts Council (OAC), an agency of the Government of Ontario. We acknowledge the support of the Canada Council for the Arts, which last year invested $153 million to bring the arts to Canadians throughout the country. This project has been made possible in part by the Government of Canada and with the support of Ontario Creates.

Cover design: Gwen North
Cover image: Shutterstock

Library and Archives Canada Cataloguing in Publication

Title: Run and gun / Eric Howling.

Names: Howling, Eric, 1956- author.

Description: Series statement: Sports stories

Identifiers: Canadiana (print) 20190097582 | Canadiana (ebook) 20190097612 | ISBN 9781459414594 (softcover) | ISBN 9781459414600 (epub)

Classification: LCC PS8615.O9485 R86 2019 | DDC jC813/.6—dc23

Published by:
James Lorimer &
Company Ltd., Publishers
117 Peter Street, Suite 304
Toronto, ON, Canada
M5V 0M3
www.lorimer.ca

Distributed in Canada by:
Formac Lorimer Books
5502 Atlantic Street
Halifax, NS, Canada
B3H 1G4

Distributed in the US by:
Lerner Publisher Services
1251 Washington Ave. N
Minneapolis, MN, USA
55401
www.lernerbooks.com

Printed and bound in Canada.
Manufactured by Marquis in Montmagny, Quebec in July 2019.
Job #174006

For Darrel, Gary and Bob

Contents

1 Warning SHOT

"Finch!" Coach Bryant's voice boomed through the gym. "You're in, Griffin."

I just about fell off the bench. I wasn't expecting Coach to call my name. There was less than a minute to play and it was just a practice game anyway. A game played on a hot day in June to see who was still in shape months after the school basketball season had ended. A chance for Coach to see who he might choose as first-stringers for the Wildcats' next season, after the long summer break.

I had been the last guy to make the Winfield College Junior Varsity team. But I'm pretty sure the only reason I didn't get cut was because Kenny Woo had broken his wrist skateboarding. Coach didn't have another guard to choose from. Bad for Kenny. Good for me.

It had been a pretty lame season, though. We went 10 and 10. Losing as many games as we won didn't get us into the playoffs. At Winfield that was big news.

Notice how I said *big* and not *good*. Winfield had a long tradition of winning. It was the first three letters of the school name, after all.

All the other Junior Wildcats teams did awesome this year. The soccer squad made it all the way to the Toronto city final. The football team took the championship with a 30–7 victory over Oakville Academy.

Winfield plays in a league with other small private schools, so its reputation is on the line every game. Being on a team at this school is kind of a big deal. Most players wear their blue Wildcat jackets every day and walk the halls like they're some kind of big shots. I don't wear mine, though. Since I wasn't a starter, I never thought I deserved it. But I kept it hung in my locker, just in case.

Our hoops team only won half our games, so Coach Bryant wasn't very happy. And he shouldn't have been. The idea was to win games, not lose them. I wasn't much help when it came to the first part. Despite trying my best, I was still a lousy dribbler and a weak passer. And as far as my three-point shot went, well, let's just say my nickname wasn't "Swish." By the end of the season my confidence was at an all-time low.

So when Coach called my name I knew this was my last chance to show I was ready to play next year. Maybe not as one of the five starters, but at least as one of the five subs who could give a first-stringer a break.

I took the inbounds pass from Rajeet Singh and

dribbled the ball up court. Scanning the floor, I searched for an open man. Tyler Dunbar was cutting into the lane. Our star centre, Tyler, is beanpole tall with long, skinny arms and legs, but always good for twenty points a game. If I could hit him with a pass, he'd have a clear path to the iron and an easy basket. I grabbed the ball in both hands and fired a hard chest pass. The ball flew toward Tyler like it had eyes. There was just one problem — Tyler's eyes were looking someplace else. The ball sailed right past him and into the hands of Brock Chilton, who was guarding him. Brock raced down court and gently laid the rock off the backboard into the hoop. I caught up to him just in time to catch the ball as it fell through the net.

"Nice pass, Griffin," Brock said, his perfect, white-toothed smile turning into a smirk. "I don't know why you're even on this team."

The whistle blew to end the game. And probably to end my future as a Wildcat.

I turned toward the locker room and started shuffling off the court. The sound of rapid footsteps bore down on me from behind.

"Finch, get changed and see me in my office," Coach snapped.

I didn't turn around. I knew bad news was coming. I just nodded and kept walking.

Run and Gun

★★★

Coach's door was half-open. I straightened the school tie under my blue sweater. I combed my fingers through my hair, which was still damp from showering. Then I knocked.

Coach peered up from behind his desk. "Take a seat, Finch."

The office was as cold as Coach's glare. The room was jail-cell small, the walls concrete grey. Feeling like an accused prisoner, I took a seat on the hard wooden chair. I sat up straight and tried not to look worried.

"The team's got to be better next season." Coach pushed back some strands of grey hair and narrowed his eyes. "A lot better."

"Yes, sir."

"We've got to make the playoffs, Finch. No two ways about it. This is *Win*field College. We don't lose."

"No, sir."

"That means some changes have to be made."

I swallowed hard. *Here it comes.*

"In my twenty years of coaching I've learned there are two ways to get better." Coach thrust a stubby finger at me. "You can either get better players, or you can make the players you have better."

I shifted nervously in my seat. Where was Coach going with this?

"Making our ten-man squad next year isn't going to be easy."

"No, sir."

"There's a lot of talent coming up. You'll be fighting it out with the rookies starting grade eight."

I nodded.

"Next fall you'll be coming back for your final year of Junior Varsity."

"Yes, sir."

"And guys in grade nine are expected to lead by example."

"Yes, sir."

"But I'm afraid the example you're setting just isn't good enough."

"No, sir."

"You do want to play for the Wildcats next season, right, Finch?"

"I sure do, Coach."

"Then you've got to improve your game."

"I'm trying my best, Coach."

"I can see that. But trying isn't enough. You've got to show me you've got game in a game. You can't just *try* to dribble, you've got to be in control when you bring the ball up court. You can't just *try* to pass, you've got to always find the open man. You can't just *try* to make the jump shot, you've got to knock it down when the clock is running out. Are you hearing me, Finch?"

"All ears, Coach."

"So work on your game this summer or —"

I looked away from Coach's hard eyes. I knew what was coming. I had to find a way to up my game.

". . . Or you'll be watching next year's Wildcat games from the stands, not the bench."

2 SHORTCUT

I slammed my locker shut and shouldered my backpack. Time to check out. Coach's warning was still spinning in my head as I started to weave my way through a sea of blue blazers. I headed for the big front doors. The arched entrance to Winfield College reflected the long history of the school. The double doors were heavy and dark, carved from wide planks of oak. The walls were smooth blocks of ancient limestone, with the date 1919 chiselled into one of the grey squares.

Most of the students were bringing home stacks of books and paper. The school year was almost toast. Just a couple exams and then I'd be out for the summer, two hot months spending my days shooting hoops at home. *Wait a minute — that was last year.* This year things were going to be different. Things had to be different. I needed a plan to amp up my game. Shooting baskets on my driveway wasn't going to be enough when I was right on the edge of being chopped from the team.

13

Run and Gun

A yellow bus was waiting in the parking lot. Most days, I'd hop on and head for home, but Brock would be on that bus. I didn't much feel like seeing his tanned face, smug smile and perfectly groomed hair. He wasn't that much better than me. Just a bit taller, a bit faster and a bit of a better shooter. Some of his jumpers actually found the net. But being just a bit better meant he was one step higher on Coach's list, and that's all it would take to bump me off the team.

I kept right on going. I cruised beside the buses, past the lot where the teachers parked. I walked along the trimmed green lawns that lined the entrance to the school.

It was a bit of a hike to my house in Riverdale. Following my usual route would take me at least an hour. I'd weave my way through safe neighbourhoods until I got to the street where I lived. But I had the munchies and wasn't sure I could wait for sixty minutes. Practice had left me with a growling stomach. I needed a snack, and the fridge at home was just the place to get it.

There was a shortcut. But it would take me through parts of town I wouldn't normally go. Sections of the city that were a little rougher. I turned right and followed my hunger.

Walking home gave me time to think. I rolled things over in my head. Coach said I needed to improve my game. I couldn't blame him for saying that.

Shortcut

Most of it was true. To be fair, I had sunk a few clutch three-point shots during the season. Still, I needed to work on my skills. One plan was to practise at the court a few blocks from my house. I could dribble, shoot a few hoops and join a pick-up game. The only problem was that most of the guys who played there were like me. That's to say pretty average. If I was ever going to get better, I had to play with guys who were a lot better.

With each passing block, the area started to look different. The paint on the homes wasn't as fresh. The fences weren't standing as straight. And the cars parked on the streets weren't as new or clean. Judging by the dust caked on the windows, some of the old beaters looked like they had been sitting there for months. Soon the houses were replaced by old apartment buildings, row after row of low-slung brick squares. And there were people everywhere. These weren't folks hurrying to downtown office meetings and stores. These were people just hanging out, sitting on benches and standing on corners. They didn't seem to have any place to go. Then I saw a few of them start to walk away. Then a few more. They were all headed to the park, to the basketball court in the middle of that park. That caught my attention. *Why the sudden attraction?* Then I saw what was drawing them like ants to sugar. A game was about to start.

Run and Gun

I moved closer. The court was surrounded by a high chain-link fence. A crowd of shouting, whistling, fist-pumping fans had their noses pressed up tight against the steel mesh. A few of them were teenage guys, my age and maybe a bit older. Some had backpacks and looked like they were on their way home from school, just like me. Some . . . I couldn't be sure they even went to school.

I hung back. This was their turf and I was just passing through. I didn't know them and they didn't know me. It seemed safer to watch from a distance.

Inside the fence I could see the two teams warming up. All the players looked like they'd be in junior or senior high. They didn't have matching uniforms — they wore a mishmash of different coloured shirts and shorts. They didn't have similar builds — they ranged from string-bean tall and lean to short and strong as a bull. I had never seen a team with so many different looking players. The Wildcats were nothing like that. Winfield was pretty white bread.

Watching the Regent Park ballers do their layups made me think I was watching a different sport. This wasn't like a Wildcats warm-up. We didn't have guys who could lay the ball in with either hand with equal skill, or sky through the air and dunk like it was no big deal. Most of us couldn't even touch the rim.

Then the game started. The pace was lightning fast, up and down the court. Jump shots from twenty feet at the top of the key. Layups from the lane under the basket. Bombs from so far away they called it downtown. After every bucket the other team would race up court and hit for another two points. It was basketball like I'd never seen before.

After one dunk, I got so caught up in the action I shouted, "Did you see that?"

Three sets of eyes turned from the fence. "What're you looking at, bro?" The biggest of the three took a step toward me. He wore a dirty white tank top, baggy shorts and high tops. He had a good six inches on me and a flat-top afro that made him seem even taller. Tattoos inked his dark, muscular arms.

"The dunk," I said, backing up. "You saw it, right?"

"What do you think we were looking at?"

"It's just that I've never seen a game played so fast. These guys are amazing."

"You've never seen run-and-gun ball before, bro?"

"Not like this."

The three friends shook their heads and laughed. "There are games like this going all day."

The shortest one was wearing a Raptors shirt. He eyed my Winfield threads suspiciously. "You don't look like you're from around here. You lost or something?"

"No, I live in Riverdale."

"Well, Riverdale," the tatted leader said, "why don't you keep walking before we charge you admission for catching a Regent Park game. Only locals get to watch for free."

I didn't want any trouble. "No problem. I have to get going anyway."

"And don't come back, unless you're here to play."

I turned and walked away. The snide laughter trailed behind me.

3 Left TURN

"Pencils down," Mrs. Booth said. The teacher stood at the front of the classroom. Her beady eyes had been scanning us like a hawk watching for rabbits. I looked up, surprised the clock had run out on me. I still had one more question to answer on my grade eight Math exam. But that wasn't bad. There were fifty multiple-choice questions. Missing one was no big deal, right?

I was heading for the door when Mrs. Booth stopped me. "You look dazed, Mr. Finch."

"Yeah, tough exam."

"You did finish every question, though. Right?"

"All but one," I said proudly.

"Ooh, that could make all the difference." Mrs. Booth winced. "Well, have a nice summer."

What did she mean, 'That could make all the difference?' I was a pretty good student. After all, it was the reason I was able to attend Winfield College, which was way too expensive for my mom to afford. Private schools like Winfield cost about as much as her whole annual salary at Walmart. Most of my classmates were sons of bankers and lawyers and real estate tycoons. But the grade eight to twelve school gave out scholarships to so-called "disadvantaged" students. I never thought of myself that way, but if it let me attend a good school like this, my mom said they could call us whatever they wanted. I got in mainly on my grades, but Mr. Hutton, the headmaster, liked that I could play hoops as well. He called me "well-rounded" or some such thing. Even so, I always felt like an outsider because I didn't come from money.

I stumbled from the classroom a lot more freaked out than when I went in. I had always got good grades in school. Now I was going to worry until my marks got sent home in the mail next month. I headed up to the second floor to empty out my locker. Math had been my last exam. Now that I was a free man, I was starting to feel better already. I jammed a couple of notebooks and some leftover basketball gear into my backpack. The bag reeked of sweat so I zipped it up quick before the smell could escape. I'm pretty sure my gym socks were the culprits.

Glancing down the hallway, I saw two of my teammates. At first I thought Tyler and Raj were heading for home just like I was. But then they took an unexpected left turn. That was the way to the gym. I decided to follow them. Wondering what was up, I watched them disappear through the gym doors.

As I got closer, I could hear balls bouncing on the court. I peered through the window in the door, but I wasn't ready for what I saw. Inside were half a dozen Wildcats taking shots at a basket. They weren't wearing their hoops uniforms, just their school pants and shirts. There was a lot of laughing and guys pounding fists after making shots. Everyone looked like they were having a good time. I pushed open the door and walked in with a big grin on my face. Suddenly, the balls stopped bouncing.

"Griffin, we didn't expect to see you here." Raj's eyes were wide, his face flushed with surprise.

"Guess I must have missed the practice notice." I smiled.

"There was no notice," Tyler said, shaking his head. "Some of next year's team just decided to get together for one last shoot-around before the summer break."

"So I should be here."

"We only invited players who are going to make the team for sure," Raj explained. "Not the other guys."

I was starting to figure things out. "You mean guys like me."

"Yeah," Brock sneered, "guys like you."

I felt my stomach somersault. I knew Brock had it in for me, but I didn't know the rest of the team felt the same way. I could feel the blood draining out of my face.

"Nothing personal, Griffin." Raj held out his hands like it was no big deal. "We think you're a good dude. We're just not sure you're good enough at basketball."

Tyler fake-smiled and offered a suggestion. "Maybe you can go to an exclusive basketball camp this summer. That's what most of us are doing. I hear Steph Curry has a good one."

Snickers spread through the gym.

"So we'll see you next September," Brock said, as he waved me out of the gym. "If you've got the guts to try out again."

My blood boiled. I wanted to say something back to Brock's face — something tough. But I wasn't sure I had the courage to face him and my other teammates again. I didn't know if I really was good enough at basketball. I bit my lip.

4 SERENA

"One-cheese-and-one-pepperoni!"

I could hear a woman ordering, words flying out of her mouth in one long stream. I peeped through the kitchen window and saw a frantic mom standing at the front counter.

"And you better hurry," she cried, waving her hands. "I've got three hungry kids waiting in my car."

"Coming right up, ma'am." Manny, the restaurant owner and my boss, turned and shouted the order back to us, "One cheese, one pepperoni!"

Serena and I rushed into action. After spreading tomato sauce and sprinkling grated cheese over two circles of white dough, I dotted one with thin slices of spicy sausage. Serena opened the red-hot oven and I slid in the two pizzas. Seven minutes later the cheese was melted and the crusts were golden brown. I took a deep breath and inhaled the Italian goodness. I rolled the sharp cutter over the twelve-inch circles and pushed them through the window.

Run and Gun

The frazzled mom stopped pacing back-and-forth and raced to the counter. She scooped up the two pizza boxes and turned to leave.

"Let me help you!" Manny said. He hurried to open the door for the woman, whose arms were now full.

Manny returned to his post behind the counter and gave us a thank-you wave.

"Another dinnertime crisis averted." Serena looked at me and laughed.

"Manny's Pizza, bringing families closer together," I kidded.

Making pizzas at Manny's was a blast. It was my first summer job, so my shifts were only between four and eight. I could ride my bike to the restaurant and never have to worry about pedalling home in the dark. The times when I got to work beside Serena were the best. She laughed at my dumb jokes and wouldn't put up with me when I got down on myself about hoops. Serena and I were a lot alike, but different at the same time. We were both brought up by our moms. Both our dads had split when we were young. We both liked playing hoops. And neither one of us could afford to dress in the latest cool clothes. Luckily, that didn't matter since we had to wear the Manny's uniform — a red shirt and green apron. It wasn't stylish but it sure made dressing easy.

On the flip side, I went to an all-boys private school

while Serena spent her days at Regent Park Junior High.

Serena picked up the conversation from when the frenzied mom rushed in. "So you don't think you're good enough to make next year's Winfield squad?"

"It's not just me who thinks that," I said, shaking my head. "Coach warned me I had to get better — or else."

"What are your chances?" Serena looked concerned.

"I'm on the bubble," I said. "Some guys are worse. But most are better. And there'll be a bunch of rookies trying out. I can't take the chance of not making it. I definitely have to up my game."

"You're going to practise all summer, right, Griffin?"

"Right." I nodded and cut some more pizza dough.

"Play a bit of pick-up down at your local court?"

"That, too."

"Well then, you should be good." Serena smiled.

"I'm not sure that's enough." I screwed up my face.

Serena could see that there was something more. "Out with it, Griffin."

"I walked home through Regent Park today and stopped to watch a pick-up game."

"And I thought you were smart," Serena joked. "Were you lost?"

"Funny, that's what some guys asked me."

"You actually talked to some of the players?"

Serena's big brown eyes widened.

"We were watching the game together. You know, until they told me to leave."

"You still have your backpack?"

"Of course," I said, innocently. "Why wouldn't I?"

Serena rolled her eyes and shook her head. "You shouldn't be hanging around Regent Park watching the games."

"You're right," I said, smiling. "I should be playing in the games at Regent Park."

Serena tilted her head at me. "Can you check in my ear? There must be something there blocking my hearing because I thought you said, 'Playing at Regent Park.'"

"I did."

"Are you out of your mind?" Serena's eyebrows shot straight up. "Those guys will eat you alive."

"I think they'll make me better."

"That's probably true, *if* they let you play."

"Why wouldn't they? I'm a baller just like them."

Serena shook her head and snorted. "You're nothing like them."

"What do you mean?"

Serena met my gaze. "Are you fast?"

"Not really. I'm more steady than fast."

"Are you quick?"

"I've been told my wit is," I wisecracked.

"And most important, can you jump?"

Serena

"I can't touch the rim yet." I raised my hand as high as I could. "But I'm hoping by next season —"

Serena cut me off. "I didn't think so. If you can't run and jump with those guys, why would they want to play with you — a slow white guy from Riverdale?"

I stopped spreading sauce on my next pizza. Serena had made a good point. If I couldn't keep up with those guys, if I couldn't score and help their team — why would they want to play with me?

5 Earn Your NAME

"Yo, Riverdale!"

It was the tattooed leader of the three-man crew that had told me to beat it from Regent Park. He was heading straight for me. He took a couple more long strides and stopped just in front of me, with his two friends just a step behind. They were all wearing grubby, mismatched muscle shirts and long shorts that hung to their knees. The leader palmed a basketball in one big hand and glared down at me. "I thought we said not to show your face here again unless you were ready to play."

My heart pounded. I wasn't sure I should be there. I wanted to act like I knew what I was doing — like this was the kind of thing I did every Saturday morning. I wanted to say something hard-nosed and confident. But all that came out of my tough-guy face was a croaky voice and two small words: "I am."

"You don't look like you're ready to play, bro. You're just wearing jeans and a T-shirt."

Earn Your Name

I didn't want to draw attention to myself coming over to Regent Park, so I wore regular clothes over top clothes to play in. "I'm wearing my gear underneath . . . see?" I quickly peeled off my shirt and pants.

"That's one fine uniform you got there," the leader mocked. "From one fine, rich-kid private school. Even the colours are the same."

I glanced down at my shirt, shorts and new kicks. Everything matched — everything was prep school blue. Even my shirt had *Winfield* spelled out in white letters across the front. I looked like I had just walked out of a Wildcats team photo from our school yearbook. What had I been thinking? I hoped wearing my uniform would show that I had game. But all it showed was that I could play in an indoor gym against spoiled white dudes. Not that I could play street ball against a bunch of locals from Regent Park.

The leader threw a question over his left shoulder. "How many guys do we have this morning, Badger?"

"Only four, Fly," his stocky teammate said. "Mailman is on his way. But Fridge has to work at his dad's auto body shop today."

The tallest player held up a long, bony finger. "So we need one more."

"I'm not an idiot, Chopper. I can count to five."

"No disrespect, Fly."

"The cage is ours in ten minutes." Badger pointed at the fenced-in court.

I could see five equally athletic hoopsters inside the cage, shooting baskets to warm up.

"Yeah, that doesn't give us much time to find someone." Fly looked up and down at my uniform one more time and sadly shook his head. "Okay, bro, you're in. Don't embarrass us."

I was about to walk through the cage door behind Fly, Badger and Chopper when someone burst in ahead of me.

"You're cutting it close, Mailman," said Chopper.

"Sorry, man. I couldn't find my lucky socks." Mailman pointed down at his mismatched red and white socks.

Fly bounced the scuffed and faded ball once on the pavement. "Listen up. We're playing the Warriors today. They're a good team, but we can take them. I'll play up front with Chopper and Badger. Mailman, you play guard with . . ." Fly tilted his head at me. "You got a name, bro?"

Griffin didn't seem like much of a name for this team. Everyone had a nickname and I wanted to fit in. "You can call me . . . *Swish*."

Badger wasn't buying it. "You can't just give yourself a nickname, man. You've got to earn it."

"None of us had handles to begin with," Chopper said. "Only after proving ourselves on the blacktop did we get a name."

Mailman agreed. "And then it was given to us."

"No one here named himself," Fly said. "Not

Chopper, not Badger, not Mailman, not even me."

I nodded sheepishly at my new teammates. "My real name is Griffin — Griffin Finch."

"Well, Finch, you're a Running Rebel today."

After a five-minute warm-up the game started. There was no ref. One of the Warriors threw the ball up at centre court for the tip-off. Fly leaped high into the blue June sky and grabbed the ball. He passed the rock back to Mailman, who raced into Warriors territory, dreadlocks flying behind him. I hung back in case there was a steal and watched my teammate weave through the other team. He did a between-the-legs dribble, a cross-over that left the defender crashing to the ground and followed with a pinpoint pass to Fly. Mailman had delivered. Fly took off from the free-throw line and sailed high above the rim. He jammed the ball through the hoop.

I had never seen anything like it except on TV. Even then, the pros seemed a step slower. This game had no whistles, no fouls, nothing to slow down the play. The pace was breakneck. I was running and sucking air already and the game was only a minute old. I didn't know if I could keep up.

The Warriors came right back at us. Their point guard raced down the court and found one of his forwards deep in the corner. Badger scooted over to try to block the shot. But he was too late. The lanky Warrior released a high, arcing shot toward the hoop. The ball hit the rim and bounced straight up. Chopper took off from the ground and snatched the ball with his long, whirling arms just before the Warriors' big man could grab it. It was an awesome rebound. Chopper shot me a look as if he was going to pass, but changed his mind and scanned across court for Mailman. I could tell he didn't trust me with the ball. I followed behind and watched him deliver another bull's-eye pass, this time to Badger, who buried a ten-foot jumper for two points.

The Warriors weren't about to roll over. This was their court just as much as it belonged to the Running Rebels. The players from both teams lived in Regent Park just blocks from here. They were playing for local bragging rights. The other Warriors forward launched a long pass down court and connected with their big man in the painted key. He made a simple layup for the deuce.

Chopper caught the ball after it dropped through the hoop and searched for a teammate to pass to.

"I'm open!" I called.

Chopper looked for Badger, then Mailman, but both were covered. He had no option. He fired a pass to me. The ball touched my hands for the first time. I tried to grip the surface but there wasn't a pebble of grain left. The ball was worn smooth by hundreds of games. My fingers had nothing to grab.

Cautiously, I moved up court. I didn't want to make a mistake. I kept my head up and dribbled slowly — too slowly. The Warriors saw that Mailman didn't have the ball and pounced. Two of them surrounded me, blocking my way forward. I was trapped. I tried to dribble out of the ambush, but a quick hand slapped the ball out of my grasp and it rolled away. One of the Warriors picked it up and raced toward our basket. He jammed it home. A mock smile that said *thanks for the two points* flashed across his face as he passed me.

I scanned the court. Chopper and Badger had their hands on their hips. Mailman and Fly were giving me the eye. I heard snickers from the fence. More and more people had gathered around the cage to watch. They had come to see some of the best players in the city. They hadn't come to watch some slow white guy in a blue Winfield uniform screw up. I hung my head in frustration. I had made a costly error. Worse, I had embarrassed my teammates.

I tried to redeem myself as the game went on, but things only got worse. The more I tried, the more I messed up. My passes were intercepted. My shots bounced off the rim. My skills had vanished like in some cruel Houdini magic trick. Fly, Chopper, Badger and Mailman did everything they could to make up for my bad play. But it wasn't enough.

When the game ended, I trailed behind my teammates as they trudged off the court. Heads were lowered and shoulders drooped. We were on the losing end of the score. The Warriors didn't leave as quietly. The air was filled with trash-talk as they stalked out of the cage. Each player took his turn rubbing it in.

"Where did you find that dude, Fly?"

"It was like you were playing a man short."

"Hope your new recruit plays again next time."

"We could use another win."

I guess I deserved the put-downs. I had pushed my way onto the Running Rebels, knowing they were better than me, hoping they would up my game. But I had let them down. Now I would never get better. Never get good enough to make the Wildcats next season.

I didn't expect anyone to stand up for me. Why would they? I started to walk away when I heard a voice behind me. "He's new, bro." I turned to see Fly standing face to face with the big man from the Warriors. "How good were you in your first game in the cage?" Fly waited for an answer, but one never came. The Warriors player only shook his head. "Just like I thought," Fly said. "I'm guessing not very."

Fly shot me a glance and nodded. "We didn't have enough players, bro. You helped us out of a jam. We couldn't have played with just four."

"Sorry I wasn't much help," I said meekly.

"You'll be better next time, Finch." Fly locked eyes with me.

"Next time?"

"Come back next Saturday. We'll be playing again. You can be a sub."

6 SMOTHER

"You look exhausted, Griffin."

Mom always worried about me. I guess that's what happens when you're the only kid of an only parent. They spend way too much time worrying about everything you do — what you eat, who you're hanging out with, where you're going. But I was fourteen and had been taller than my mom for a year. I didn't need someone watching my every move.

"I've been playing hoops."

"I can see that." Mom nodded from the other side of the kitchen. "Your uniform is all sweaty. You must have been playing hard."

"Hardest game I ever played, Mom." I pulled a box of apple juice from the fridge and started chugging.

"It's nice there's a park close by where you can play with your friends."

"That's not where I was playing." Oops. I wanted to keep the location a secret and looked away.

"Why wouldn't you play there? It's just down the street."

"The guys that play there aren't good enough."

"What about practising with Tyler and Raj and Brock?" Now her hands were on her hips. "Are they good enough for you?"

"They're only a bit better than I am. And they don't want to play with me." I threw up my hands in frustration. "I need to up my game so I can be better than them. And I can't do that if I just play the kids around here."

"Then where did you play?" Her eyes narrowed with concern.

"Regent Park." I shrugged like it was no big deal.

"Can't you play somewhere closer?"

I rolled my eyes. "I'm going to shoot some hoops."

"Not at Regent Park I hope," Mom said quickly.

"No, on our driveway." I pursed my lips hard. "Is that close enough for you?"

I grabbed my ball from the garage and bounced it a couple of times. It was good to feel the pebbled surface of a new ball in my hand. I stepped into the sunlight and dribbled toward the basket at the side of the driveway. I backed in like I was protecting the ball from a Warriors defender and then turned to release a jumper. The orange sphere floated through the air in a perfect arc before dropping through the net. *Swish*.

Why couldn't I have done that in the game? But I hadn't. All I had done was cause the Running Rebels to lose. I couldn't let that happen again. I had to practise — even if I was tired. And the best place to practise was in private, right here at home. I didn't want Fly or Chopper or any of my other new teammates to see me flub a pass or blow an open shot again.

First, I had to get in better shape. The pace of the game had been so fast I spent half my time bent over, sucking wind. I was wrong to think I was in shape from playing with the Wildcats. I could see where the Running Rebels had gotten their name. They would blow by me like I was standing still. The Warriors had been just as athletic, just as speedy. I ran up and down the driveway doing wind sprints, ten lengths at a time.

Then I picked up the ball and started dribbling up and down the driveway. Right hand, left hand, between my legs, behind my back, cross-over, stutter-step. It wasn't always smooth, and sometimes the ball skittered away. But I kept at it. The only way I was going to make it second nature was to repeat it again and again.

Finally, I turned my attention to the net that hung ten feet in the air above me. I started in close with some easy layups. Then I moved back a few steps at a time. I hit five-foot hook shots, ten-foot jumpers and twenty-foot set shots from wide on the side.

After a couple of hours in the hot sun, my arms felt like rubber. That was enough. For today.

7 Two POINTS

"Hey, Winfield, where's the clown suit?" Badger held a ball in the crook of his arm and gave my shirt and shorts the once-over. I wasn't wearing my all-blue Winfield uniform like last week. I wasn't going to make that mistake again.

"Why is he here?" Mailman pointed a finger at me.

"Because I asked him," Fly said. "Because we need him."

"Need him like a bad cold," Badger snickered. He reached out and pounded fists with Mailman.

Chopper nodded. "Yeah, we've got the regular crew here. All five of us, even Fridge."

"It's good to have a sub," Fly said, giving Chopper the eye. I could see he didn't like his teammates questioning him. "Other teams have one. And from what I saw last game, you could have used one, too."

Chopper hung his head and nodded. "It was a tough game, man."

Badger smacked the ball hard on the asphalt and

caught it firmly in both hands. "Okay, Fly, but I'll tell you this — no guy from Riverdale is starting a game for the Running Rebels here in Regent Park."

Even though it was morning, it was baking hot. Drips of sweat were rolling down the Rebels' faces — and that was just from the warm-up. I sat on the metal bench by the fence and watched the opening tip. The guys the Running Rebels were playing, the Hawks, looked like a strong team. They won the tip-off and raced straight down court at Mailman and Badger. Passing the ball around fast, they zipped the rock to all five teammates before finding their tall centre under the net, who laid it in for an easy basket. This was going to be another tough game.

The Hawks' defence kept the pressure on. Badger brought the ball up court and tried to find Fridge in the middle. His pass was high and sailed over the big man. Badger shook his head in frustration. The Hawks swooped back into our zone, five men strong. A quick pass to the corner and a forward drained a long bomb. The Hawks looked like they were running away with the game.

That's when Fly took matters into his own hands. After Mailman dribbled the ball into the Hawks' zone, Fly faked-out his defender, leaped into the clear and looked for the ball. Mailman saw Fly was open and delivered a letter-perfect bounce pass right into his hands. Another Hawks defender blocked his path to the basket but that didn't stop Fly. He took off like a jet and powered right up and over the Hawk, hovering high over the hoop before jamming home the rock.

It was an awesome move. Fly still had fire in his eyes as he ran back and pointed a taunting finger at the dude he had beaten. It only took a few minutes for me to see why Fly was the leader.

The rest of the Running Rebels picked up on Fly's in-your-face attitude. When the Hawks came down court again, Badger was all over the ball handler, hounding him every step of the way. When a Hawks teammate received a pass, Chopper's long arms whirled in front of him like helicopter blades. It made it impossible for the Hawks player to pass the ball. That's when Mailman swooped in and stole the rock. He dribbled the ball up court and looked for Fridge on the low post near the net. Fridge was there. He was always there. Fridge was so big and heavy, no one could push him out of the way. Mailman snapped a pass to him. Fridge clutched the ball in his beefy hands. He spun toward the basket and put up a soft shot that hit the iron and dropped. Another bucket. The game was tied.

The Hawks were shocked. They called a timeout and huddled together under their basket to regroup. Fly raised his hand and called the Running Rebels over to the bench where I sat.

"Mailman and Badger, nice work handling the ball. Chopper and Fridge, awesome job in their zone."

Two Points

Then without a pause Fly said, "Finch, you're in for Mailman."

"Say what?" Mailman's eyes bugged out of his head.

"You heard me," Fly said to Mailman. "Take a breather. You'll be stronger at the end when we really need you."

"I thought we were trying to win this game," Badger said.

"We are, bro."

Badger wasn't the only one puzzled by Fly's move to put me in. By now a crowd had gathered around the cage. Old men out for walks, high-school ballers waiting their chance to play and young kids all peered through the chain-link fence. I shot a nervous glance at them.

"There goes the game," an old timer wearing a Raptors ball cap said.

A teen covered his eyes in mock horror. "I don't think I can watch, man."

Fly waved the Rebels back onto the court. As Mailman sat down, I stood up. My knees felt weak, my hands shook, my heart pounded. I was as jumpy as a cat in a dog pound. I had practised hard all week, but was it enough? Most of my teammates didn't think so. Chopper and Fridge shot dagger-eyes at me. Badger gave me a death stare. I could pretty much read their minds. One mistake and I was done.

A Hawks guard dribbled the ball over the mid-court line. I backpedalled, scanning for the position of his teammates. I saw a Hawks forward cutting to the top of the key. I checked the guard's eyes. He was going to pass! I cut to my left, predicting the path of his throw. He released the ball and I lunged. I blocked the pass but skidded hard along the blacktop. I bounced up and grabbed the rock. Blood trickled from my knee as I raced into the Hawks' zone. There were no defenders. The lane was clear. I made one last dribble before driving to the hoop. The ball spun off the backboard and dropped through the iron. Two points.

I raced back to our zone and waited. The Hawks guard brought the ball up court again. This time he was slow, not so sure of himself. I jumped in front of him, crouching low with my hands stretched out. He was rattled. The next dribble bounced off his foot and rolled along the asphalt. I scooped up the ball and dashed toward the Hawks' basket with Badger cruising beside me. We zipped the ball back and forth, leaving the defender only able to guess who would shoot. I leaped in the air and released the jumper. The ball kissed off the backboard and fell sweetly through the hoop. Two more points.

I didn't pump my fist. Didn't shout. Didn't point a taunting finger. After my meltdown last week, I was just glad to be helping the team. I didn't expect my teammates to be impressed. To them I was still the slow white guy from Winfield College with no street cred.

Suddenly, Badger and Chopper were coming at me from one side. Fly and Fridge rushed at me from the other. Their arms were raised. I froze. Were they glad or mad? Seconds later I had my answer. Badger and Chopper launched themselves in the air to deliver massive chest-bumps to me that just about slammed me to the ground. Fly and Fridge reached up for high-fives. Even Mailman left the bench and was on his feet punching the air with his fist.

"You've got some game, Riverdale." A huge grin spread across Chopper's face.

Badger nodded. "Every time you touch the ball you score two points."

Fridge's deep voice boomed like an announcer, "Two points for Riverdale."

"That's it," Fly said. "From now on we'll call you TP."

I grimaced. Why did my teammates want to call me Toilet Paper? Did they think I was that bad?

"Why the frown, bro?" Fly asked.

"I'm not sure Toilet Paper is such a good nickname."

"Toilet Paper?" Fly doubled over in laughter. "TP stands for Two Points, bro. Two Points."

I had to smile. And not just because I had earned a nickname. I realized I was learning to play better by just watching the guys on the team. How to thread a perfect pass like Mailman. How to be a dangerous dribbler like Badger. How to play crazy-hands defence like Chopper. How to be a tank under the hoop like Fridge. And how to slash your way to the basket like Fly. I didn't need to go to an expensive summer basketball camp. I was attending Camp Running Rebels right here in Regent Park.

8 SCHOOL'S OUT

Water had never tasted so good.

I finished slurping my share of the city's water supply, ice-cold liquid pouring down my dry throat. I had to replace all the sweat that had drenched my shirt while we played under the hot July sun. But it had been worth it. We had just beaten the Spurs, one of the best teams in the summer league. I raised my head from the fountain just outside the cage.

"Yo, TP!" Mailman called out as he walked toward the street. "Same time next week, man."

I wiped the last cool drops from my lips. "I'll be here."

My mouth widened into a big goofy grin. I was still the worst player on the team, but I had held my own. I had managed to score eight points and set up Fridge, Chopper and Fly for a bunch more. And the best part was that we had won. I felt like I was part of the team.

Badger, Mailman and Fridge pounded fists with me before they headed out. Fly was the last to get a drink and stood up from the fountain. "You're getting better, TP."

"You guys make me better. You can all run faster, jump higher and shoot better than me. But I get better just by trying to keep up."

"Soon you'll be just as good, bro."

I shook my head, not believing Fly for a second.

"Well, almost as good." Fly's laugh showed a mouthful of bright white teeth.

We started walking through the park. It was nothing like the green spaces of Riverdale. The cement path was stained and cracked. Coffee cups and pop cans had spilled onto the ground from the garbage bins. An old man in dingy clothes lay asleep on the well-worn bench we were passing.

I turned my attention from the dozing man back to Fly. "You guys must have an awesome time playing for the Regent Park school team."

"Are you kidding?" Fly laughed again. "You think we play for Regent? Most of us don't even go to school full-time anymore. Chopper is the only one who shows up every day. And that's only because his mom makes him."

I stopped dead in my tracks. "So you don't go to school?"

"Not all the time, man." Fly shook his head and gave me a pitiful look. "I go just enough for them to let me play hoops."

School's Out

"How come?"

"I didn't see the point, bro. School isn't the way I'm going to make it out of Regent Park."

I couldn't imagine not going to school, or needing another way to avoid spending the rest of my life working at Manny's. We came to a red light and I stopped. But Fly kept walking, dodging cars as they drove by.

"So what do you do when you're not in school?" I asked when I caught up to Fly on the other side of the street.

"I mainly hang out here with Badger and Mailman, shooting hoops."

After a couple of blocks Fly stopped and tilted his head. "This is where I live, TP."

I had been listening so closely to Fly's story that I hadn't paid much attention to the neighbourhood. I looked at the apartment building in front of us. Some of the old bricks were crumbling. Flakes of paint were peeling off the windowsills and white graffiti was scrawled along the side. A sad-eyed man and woman sat on the front steps, taking sips from a paper bag.

"See you next game, bro," said Fly.

We pounded fists and Fly bounded up the steps two at a time. He dodged the rumpled couple huddled on the steps and disappeared behind the front door. I noticed that tape held together a crack in the glass.

I turned and headed home. Walking along the

busy street, I noticed the traffic and people and buildings more than I ever had before. After a while the pounding rap music from cruising cars turned into the quiet idling of sedans. And the drab brick apartments turned into houses with clipped hedges along green leafy streets.

I stopped at the end of the driveway in front of my own house. It was the smallest one on the block. But it had a new coat of paint and the lawn smelled of freshly mowed grass. I walked inside wondering if Fly had a full fridge of food waiting for him like I did.

9 Extra TOPPINGS

"Couple of Hawaiians!" Manny called back to the kitchen. I jumped off my stool and flew into action. I spread handfuls of ham and pineapple over the round of pizza dough.

Working Friday nights was all good. Good because Manny's was busy. The place was packed with starving college and high-school kids desperate to stuff their faces with hot hunks of 'za. Good because a busy restaurant meant I was busy, and I liked that. In the six weeks since school had ended, I had been working almost every night. Some shifts hardly anyone came through the door and I'd be sitting in the back bored out of my mind. I'd rather be rolling dough than twiddling my thumbs. And Friday nights were also good because I got to spend time with Serena.

"Why are those pies taking so long, Griffin?" Manny asked. "Are they flying in from Hawaii or what?"

"No, sir, just coming out of the oven now." Serena handed me two boxes. I sliced the cheesy discs before pushing them through the delivery window to Manny.

"Another satisfied customer," I said, hopping back on my stool.

"Friday nights you're on that stool every chance you get." Serena wrinkled her brow.

"I'm saving my legs."

"For what? Are you running a marathon tomorrow morning?"

"No, I'm playing hoops. And if I stand up all night I won't be able to run or jump."

"You can jump?" Serena kidded.

"More of a hop really, but I'm working on it." It was a bad joke, but I wasn't very good at talking to girls. I didn't have a sister to practise on. Since Winfield was an all-boys school there weren't any girls there, either. Serena made it easy, though. She was always quick with a smile or a wisecrack.

"So where's the game?" she asked.

"I'm playing with the Running Rebels down at Regent Park."

Serena's jaw dropped. "The Running Rebels are one of the best teams down there. Fly Davis is a one-of-a-kind player."

"You know him?"

"Everyone knows Fly. He's a legend down at the park. He was the star of the junior high team too, until . . ."

"Until he quit going to class?" I asked.

"Yeah, something like that."

"He told me the teachers didn't care."

"They didn't care to get punched, more like it," Serena said. "Rumour had it that Fly and Coach got into a fight — fists and the whole thing. Something about how much playing time Coach was giving Fly. Or not giving him. They smoothed things over but Fly quit going to some of his classes after that. He figured hoops was the only thing he was good at."

"Well, he is good at it."

Serena nodded. "The best."

I stood so close to Serena that I could smell her shampoo. We kneaded pizza dough into circles ready for the next order.

"When's your next game?" Serena asked, not looking up.

"We play most Saturday mornings in the cage."

"Maybe I'll come down sometime and check you . . . I mean . . . check *the team* out."

My throat got a little dry. I wasn't sure what to say. Nobody had ever wanted to see me play before. Especially a girl. I nodded.

I heard the door to the restaurant open followed by footsteps. "Give me a deluxe with all the toppings," a guy's voice said. "And make it fast."

I know that voice, I thought. I peered through the open window. Brock and Tyler from the Wildcats stood at the counter. I jumped back out of view. I didn't want them to know I was working at a pizza joint for the summer.

"That's one deluxe, Griffin!" Manny shouted back at me.

I froze. Maybe if I didn't say anything, Brock would think another Griffin was working here. I zipped my lips.

"Griffin, are you listening?" Manny shouted again.

I didn't want to get fired. I had to say something. "Coming right up!"

"Finch, is that you?" Brock called out.

I knew Manny liked us to be friendly to the customers. I stuck my head in the kitchen window and gave a small wave.

"Nice uniform," Brock smirked. He pointed at my red shirt and green apron.

"You look like a cartoon, Finch," Tyler cracked.

I had to change the subject. "What are you guys up to?"

"Nothing much," Brock said. "Just got my dad to drive us down here in our new Porsche. I'd invite you for a ride. But it looks like you're busy doing something we never have to do — work." He shook his head and snickered.

Serena pushed a hot pizza through the kitchen window. "One deluxe, with extra toppings for Griffin's *friends.*"

Manny handed the cardboard box to Brock.

"See ya, Finch," Brock called over his shoulder as he and Tyler headed out the door. "We don't want to waste our time here."

Once they were gone, Serena rolled her eyes. "So they're your Wildcats teammates?"

"Yup." I sighed.

"I can see why you'd rather play for the Running Rebels," Serena said. "The Rebels are tough, but they respect their teammates."

"At least they're gone now." I slid back on to my stool.

"But they should have bought a drink to go with that pizza." Serena chuckled.

I raised an eyebrow. "You didn't?"

"I sure did." Serena's eyes danced with mischief. "Their pizza has an extra handful of burning hot chili peppers on it."

10 The Park AFTER DARK

The ring of fans stood three deep around the cage — a pack of hooting, hollering, hand-clapping fans. Their shadowed faces were lit up by the bright lights shining overhead. Everyone from the neighbourhood had come out to watch Hoops in the Park after Dark — the tournament held at the end of every summer.

It was hard to believe I was playing in the noon-until-midnight tournament. It seemed like years ago that I wasn't invited to play in a pick-up game with the Wildcats at the end of school. But that was just two months ago, back in June. Now it was late August and I was playing with some of the best ballers in Regent Park. With players who also happened to be some of the best ballers in the city. And I wasn't a charity case, either. It wasn't as if Fly and the rest of the team felt sorry for me. Pity didn't get me on the team. And it didn't keep me on the team. Fly would never have stood for that. Week after week I had worked my butt off. My play got better and better as the summer went on. Now Badger, Chopper, Mailman and Fridge weren't my enemies, they were my friends. Now I was a regular on the team. I was a real Running Rebel.

Playing in front of a crowd this big was a huge rush. My heart was still pounding from the semi-final game we had just won.

"Yo, TP!" Fly called out as we paraded out of the cage. The cheers of the crowd were still ringing in our ears. "It's a good thing you were able to make it today, bro. We couldn't have won these three games without you."

"Yeah, we were worried when you didn't show at first," Chopper kidded. "Thought your mom might not let you play after dark."

Badger pulled his best scary face. "You know, Regent Park being such a dangerous place and all."

"Very funny," I said. "I can play whenever I want. TP's mom doesn't tell him when he can shoot hoops."

"That's good, because the championship game doesn't start for another hour. It's at eleven o'clock," Mailman said. "And we're playing in it."

I was glad we had a break. It had been a long, hot day. The tournament had started with sixteen teams and now we were down to the final two. The Running Rebels had already taken care of the Bucks, Spurs and Warriors. Now we were up against the Celtics, a team we hadn't beat all summer.

I plunked down on the grass with Fly and the rest

of my teammates. Dusk was falling, but we sat just steps from the bright lights of the cage. I pulled on a bottle of lime Gatorade, hoping to suck back some energy for the big game. I looked around the park. The sun was setting like a glowing orange ball behind the old apartment buildings. There were families of all ages hanging out, laughing and having a good time. Music was thumping from the huge speakers that had been set up near the cage to entertain fans between games. An ice cream truck was selling drumsticks to kids on the street. Regent Park didn't look very scary to me.

Crack! . . . Crack! Crack! Crack!

Loud bursts blasted through the peaceful night air.

"What the hell was that?" Fridge shouted, his eyes popping wide.

Badger's head whipsawed. "Firecrackers?"

"Maybe a car tire exploded?" Chopper guessed.

Fly shook his head. "You've got it all wrong, man. Those were gunshots."

I froze. I didn't know what to do.

Moms and dads were screaming to find their kids. Packs of fans were rushing away from the cage as fast as they could. There was the sound of sirens, and it was getting closer. Panic filled the park.

"Don't worry!" Fly said calmly. "It's probably just a drug deal gone bad."

"Just a drug deal?" I fired back. "Someone's shooting!"

The Park After Dark

"Happens all the time, bro."

Black and white police cars came flying around the corner and drove right up on the grass. Sirens blared as red and blue lights flashed in the growing darkness. One cop jumped out and rushed to help the man who had been shot. Two more officers with raised pistols raced by, chasing the fleeing man with the gun.

That's when I decided to take off. I wasn't going to wait for more gunshots to be fired, for someone else to take a bullet. I didn't want to hang around to find out what happened. Didn't want to be caught in a crossfire between the police and a gun-crazed drug dealer.

So I ran. I flew through the shadows of the park, dodging people left and right. And I kept running until I reached Riverdale, where I sprinted up my quiet street and into the safety of my house. Locking the door of my room, I collapsed on the bed and stared at the ceiling — my heart pounding, my chest heaving, my whole body shaking with fear.

11 Last NIGHT

On our last night of the summer working at Manny's, Serena seemed quiet. She kept her head down and avoided my eyes as she grabbed a handful of green pepper for a veggie pizza. "I bet you've never seen anything like last night in Riverdale," she said.

I arched an eyebrow. "You're talking about what went down in Regent Park?"

Serena nodded.

"How do you know about that?"

"I was there, Griffin. I saw the whole thing."

I knew she meant the shooting, but I was happy she was also there to watch our games. "So you saw me . . . I mean the Running Rebels play?"

"Uh-huh." Serena gave me a shy smile. "I was outside the cage with all the other fans. Hoops in the Park after Dark is a tradition. It's like the official end of summer. It means it won't be long before we have to head back to class. I wouldn't miss it."

I could feel my face flush, so I took a swig of water

to calm down. Blushing wasn't cool.

"You're not half bad for a slow white guy." Serena grinned and lightly punched me in the arm. "I could probably take you one-on-one, but still . . ."

"Get real," I joked, returning the tap on her arm. "You wouldn't stand a chance against me. Fly is always copying my moves."

Serena rolled her eyes. "I know you're kidding, but you really have gotten a lot better."

"And I can thank Fly for that. He gave me the chance to play. The chance to pass and shoot alongside the Running Rebels. Just being on the same court as those guys has upped my game. Regent Park has been good for me."

"Too bad it wasn't good for everyone." Serena pursed her lips in frustration.

"So did you see what happened last night?" I asked.

"I took off as soon as I heard the first shot," Serena said. "I'm not stupid. I'd rather be alive than dead, thank you very much."

"I'm glad you got out of there when you did," I said. "I'd hate to think of anything bad happening to you."

Serena paused and met my eyes before continuing. "I didn't stick around waiting for the cops to show. But I did hear about it the next day. Everyone was talking about it. The city is trying to improve RP. But there are still drugs, guns and gangs, just like anywhere in the city."

"I know that this stuff happens. That's why my mom wanted to get me into my school."

"No kidding," Serena scoffed. "Your school is so squeaky clean it's like a big kindergarten for teenagers."

I shook my head and smiled. Partly because Serena's description of Winfield was bang on. Partly because I was going to miss her. When we first met at Manny's, we'd hardly said a word to each other. But now we could talk about anything. I never thought a girl could be one of my best friends, but that's what Serena was now.

My mom wouldn't let me keep working when school started, which was in just a couple of days. She said I had to concentrate on studying, that I had to keep getting good marks so I could stay at Winfield.

It was getting near eight and our shift was almost over. I put a leftover pizza in a box to take home. Then I took off my green apron and hung it up for the last time.

Serena wouldn't look at me. She kept spreading vegetables, even though there were no customers. "You trying out for the Wildcats this season?"

I nodded. "That's the plan."

"You've been playing with the best all summer, Griffin. I could tell you had upped your game, that you could hold your own with the Running Rebels. From what I saw, you should make the team, no problem."

"Thanks, that means a lot coming from you."

Last Night

I wondered if this would be the last chance I got to stand next to Serena. If I'd have to wait a whole year to see her again. I moved closer. "And what about you? Starting point guard for Regent Park Junior High again?"

Serena turned and gave me a quick hug. Her face brightened and looked as determined as ever. "You know it."

12 Rookie SQUAD

A sharp whistle cut through the stale gym air. Coach Bryant stood at centre court wearing his blue Winfield tracksuit and white hoop kicks. A clipboard was in his hands. "Okay, everyone, bring it in."

The gym went silent. The dribbling stopped. The shooting ended. All the players trying out for the Wildcats gathered around Coach. It was a real mash-up of veterans and rookies, tall and short, muscly and skinny. Everyone was dressed in practice gear — mismatched tank tops and long shorts. No Winfield blue uniforms would be given out until the final team had been selected.

Standing in one group were the returning vets: Brock Chilton, Tyler Dunbar, Rajeet Singh, Jaxen Alexander and Kenny Woo, who was back from sitting out because of his broken wrist. Then there was a cluster of new guys trying to make the team. I stood in between the two groups.

"Let's split into two squads." Coach scanned the

keen faces around him. "I know a lot of you guys spent the summer at big-name basketball camps learning from star NBA players."

"You know it, Coach," Tyler said. "Nothing but the best."

Coach nodded. "So I expect to see some real improvement."

"Don't worry, Coach," Brock said, as he pounded fists with Tyler. "If you didn't spend a month at an elite camp, you won't have a chance against us." Brock turned and smirked at me. "Especially if you had to work all summer, like at a pizza joint."

"I'm looking forward to seeing how you've upped your game, Brock," Coach said. "And to judge how all you veterans have improved, I want to see you play against the new recruits."

"What about me, Coach?" I asked, wondering where I fit in.

"Finch, you play with the new guys — the rookies trying to make the team."

"Yeah, trying . . ." Brock snickered.

What? I wasn't a starter last year, but I wasn't a rookie either. Did I really belong with the new guys? I knew Brock didn't think I had any game, but it didn't seem like Coach had much confidence in me, either. I sighed and joined the rookies. They all looked dazed, not knowing where to play or who to cover. I couldn't get sucked into their confusion. I had to play my own game. I had to show Coach he had made a mistake.

"There are ten spots up for grabs on the team," Coach said. "Every one has to be earned, whether you're a vet or rookie." Coach tossed the ball to Brock. "Let's go, Wildcats, game on."

Brock brought the ball into our zone. A cocky smile was smeared across his face. He thought this was going to be easy — like taking candy from a bunch of rookie babies. I knew he wasn't a great dribbler and waited for him to look down at the ball. That's when I rushed him. I jumped in his path just like Chopper had shown me. My hands spun around him like the blades of a helicopter. Brock panicked. The ball slipped away from his fingers and I grabbed it. Kenny chased me, but I was too far ahead. I flew toward the basket and cushioned the ball off the backboard for an easy layup.

I wasn't done. Tyler stood behind the baseline with the ball, his eyes moving left and right, looking for an open teammate. I guessed he'd try to pass to Jaxen like always. He did. As soon as he released the ball, I leaped in front of Jaxen just like Badger would have done. I intercepted the rock and, in one motion, took a fifteen-foot jumper. The ball spun high through the air and hit nothing but net on the way down. After less than a minute the score was Griffin 4, Wildcats Veterans 0.

The whistle blew. "Timeout!" Coach ran his fingers through his hair as both teams circled around him.

"What's going on out there? You call yourselves veterans? Brock, you have to work on your dribbling. Tyler, you have to look before you pass. You guys know better than that."

"It won't happen again, Coach," Tyler said, hanging his head.

Brock nodded. "I guess we're a little rusty since camp."

Coach gave his whistle a short burst and flipped the ball back to Brock. "Okay, let's get out there and try again. No mistakes this time."

Brock dribbled the ball into our rookie zone for a second time. Now his head was up. His hotshot smile was gone. Brock's eyes scanned the floor, looking for an open teammate. I saw Tyler move into the paint under the basket. He raised his hand to signal Brock that he was in the clear. But I wasn't going to let him just stand there. I remembered how Fridge used his big body to push other players away from the basket. If he could do it, so could I. Even though Tyler was taller, I inched my way forward, forcing him to take a few steps away from the hoop. By the time Brock passed him the ball, Tyler was out of range to make a simple layup. He had to spin and take a hook shot from outside the key. It was a shot he hadn't practised. The ball clanged against the rim and bounced away. My feet left the floor and I reached high to pull down the rebound.

Moving up court, I started dribbling just like

Run and Gun

Mailman — between my legs, behind my back, left-hand, right-hand. I saw a rookie teammate cutting into the middle and I delivered the mail — a perfect bounce pass right into his hands. He snagged the ball and looked for the basket, but Tyler's long octopus arms waved all over him.

I had to get open. I raced to the top of the key and called for the pass. "Here!"

Grabbing the ball, I drove to the basket just like Fly. Nothing ever stopped him. Nothing was going to stop me. I took to the air, skying above Brock's outstretched hands. I shifted the rock from my left to right hand in mid-flight and banked it off the backboard. The ball fell silently through the iron and into the mesh.

Brock narrowed his eyes as I dashed by. I gave him a half-smile and raced back to my position at the other end of the court, waiting for the veterans' next rush.

Twenty minutes later Coach blew his whistle for the last time. The old-boy Wildcats had made a comeback. Tyler picked up his game and showed why he was one of the best players in the league. But it wasn't enough. The rookie team had won by two points.

The veteran squad was playing down their loss.

"It's no big deal," Tyler said. Beads of sweat poured down his face. "I wasn't even trying that hard."

"Yeah," Brock chipped in, still out of breath. "We pretty much let you guys win."

The veteran five had lost to a bunch of rookies, plus a guy no one thought would make the team. I walked off the court wondering if Coach had noticed.

"Finch," Coach called from behind. "I don't know what kind of camp you went to this summer, but it must have been a good one."

13 Surprise MOVE

The Wildcats' first game of the season was just an hour away. The team from Markham Prep would be pulling up in their bus any minute.

I couldn't wait to suit up in Winfield colours. And not just as a back-up player sitting on the bench. This year I'd be the starting guard alongside Kenny Woo. I walked into the gym and headed for the locker room, passing by Coach Bryant's office on the way. His door was shut and his blinds were pulled tight. That seemed odd. Coach usually kept both wide open. I couldn't see inside, but I could hear Coach's gruff voice. "I'm surprised," he said. "This changes everything."

I pushed through the door into the locker room, scratching my head. Something was going down but I didn't know what. I took a seat and scanned the room. Every player was there putting on his gear. *Brock, Jaxen, Kenny, Raj . . . wait a minute . . . rewind. Where's Tyler?*

The door swung open. Coach marched in, the tall, lanky figure of Tyler a step behind. Tyler's eyes were downcast, as if he was searching the floor for something he had lost.

When Coach said, "Listen up," the room fell silent. All eyes zeroed in on him. "I've got an announcement to make."

I held my breath.

"Tyler won't be playing in today's game," Coach said.

"Why not?" The same question escaped from everyone's lips.

Coach glanced around the room. "In fact, he won't be playing in any more games for Winfield College."

My mind raced. *Is Tyler sick? Is he getting kicked out of school?*

Coach turned to his star player. "Why don't you tell your teammates what's going on."

Tyler paused before talking. At first I wasn't sure he'd be able to get the words out. Even as he started to speak, he kept his head down and didn't look anyone in the eye.

"I'm moving to New York City," he mumbled. "The company my mom works for is promoting her to head office right away. We're leaving later today." Tyler finally raised his head and searched the room. "I'm sorry, guys."

"How come I didn't know?" Brock blurted out. "I thought we were friends."

"I couldn't tell anyone. My mom had to keep it a secret because she didn't know if she would get the job."

Jaxen turned to Coach. "What are we going to do?"

"Yeah," Kenny said. "Tyler's our best player."

"I know." Coach pursed his lips. "This is a big blow to our team. We were counting on Tyler to lead us this season. For this afternoon's game Rajeet will start at centre."

"Me?" Raj's eyes popped. "But I've never played centre before, Coach."

"Well, you will today."

***

The year before, the Markham Mavericks had finished in last place. We had beaten them twice during the season. So I thought we still had a chance against them. Hey, maybe they wouldn't even notice that Tyler was missing from the line-up.

For the first few minutes we held our own. Both teams scored a couple of buckets. I even set up Raj for an easy two-point layup under the hoop. Things were looking good. Then I saw one of the Markham players point and shout, "They don't have their big man!"

Suddenly, the plodding Mavericks turned into the blazing fast Mavericks. They sensed we had a weakness and they were going to take advantage of it. The Mavs raced down the court every time they got the ball. Their passes were crisp. Their shooting was on target. Their baskets mounted up. They were leaving us in their dust.

Worst of all, the Markham players started to trash-talk.

"Your team is nothing without Stretch," said their short guard, running by me.

"Win-field? More like Loser-field," called a voice from their bench.

The harder we tried, the worse it got. Coach called timeouts and tried to get us back on track. We tried different combinations of players. Sometimes Brock played centre instead of Raj, sometimes Jaxen. Nothing worked.

I did everything I could to even the score. I knocked down passes, dove for loose balls, made some pinpoint passes and even hit a few threes from outside. But we were falling further and further behind. By the end of the game we were down by fifteen points. It wasn't even close.

No one said much back in the locker room. Then Jaxen broke the silence. "That was brutal, man."

Brock slammed his locker shut. "Totally. If the Mavericks can beat us, just imagine what the good teams will do."

Kenny shook his head, disgusted by his own play. "We may not win a game all year."

I shot a glance at Coach Bryant. He was standing by himself away from the players. He looked worried. I had never seen his forehead so wrinkled. I knew the school was putting a lot of pressure on him to win this season. Finally, he took a few steps toward us. "That was a tough game, guys." He pushed back a handful of grey hair that had been mussed during the game. "But we can't give up just because Tyler is gone."

"He's left some big shoes to fill," Kenny said.

Jaxen picked up a high top and tossed it in his locker. "And all our feet are too small."

"We need another star player," Brock said.

"We have to play with the nine guys we've got," Coach said. "Look around this room. You're the best players in the school. There's no one else to choose from. No one else is going to save us. No one even applied for the second scholarship we give out each year to disadvantaged players."

Why hadn't I thought of that sooner? That was the same scholarship they gave me.

"I might know someone, Coach," I piped up.

"Someone from that big-name camp you went to?"

"Yeah, something like that."

4 The OFFER

It was the first time I'd been back to Regent Park. My summer playing hoops with the Running Rebels in the cage was over. I had no reason to return. Besides, my mom freaked out when she heard the news about the shooting in the park. There was no way she was going to let me get mixed up in that. So that Saturday morning I had to sneak out of the house.

While some parts of Regent Park had been fixed up, the area where Fly lived still had that faded, yesterday feel. I felt like I was in a movie that had been filmed fifty years ago. The houses, corner stores and streets all looked old, except for a few flashy cars that were pumping out heavy bass.

It didn't take long to find the rundown apartment building I was searching for. I walked up the cement steps and through the front door with the taped-up glass. A strange odour filled the entrance, a nose-holding mixture of old carpet, wet dog hair and boiled cabbage. Trying not to breathe, I scanned the row of mailboxes for apartment numbers, then ran up the stairs to the third floor. The long corridor had only a few bulbs burning to brighten the hallway. I checked the numbers on the doors and stopped when I came to 306.

I knocked three times. The wooden door creaked open and a woman who had to be Fly's mom stood in front of me. She eyed me then called over her shoulder. "Freddie, it's for you!"

When I heard Fly's real name I grinned. Now I knew why everyone called him by his nickname. I wondered what Fly thought of me hightailing it out of the park that crazy night a few weeks ago. He might have thought I was some kind of scared chicken. He might not want to see me.

"Yo, Riverdale."

Fly flashed his white-tooth grin, reached out to pound fists and waved me inside. The apartment was small, but clean and sunny. We sat on an old, comfy couch in front of a TV showing a college hoops game.

"Didn't think I'd see you around here again," Fly said, shaking his head. "I didn't know you could run that fast."

"Sticking around didn't seem like a smart thing to do," I said.

"You mean the gunshots after the drug deal?"

I nodded.

"That kind of thing goes on all the time in Regent Park." Fly shrugged. "No big deal. And like I said, it's just too bad my bro wasn't there."

I lowered my voice. "The one with the gun?"

"Yeah, Jamal. He runs with the RP gang."

I glanced around the apartment. "Does he live here, too?"

"Not anymore." Fly gave his head half a shake. "He's doing time for armed robbery."

My eyes widened. I didn't understand how life could be like that. Riverdale wasn't a rich part of town either. But I'd never seen a shootout in a park. I'd never seen a gun. And kids' brothers weren't in prison.

Fly shifted in his seat. "So did you get lost on your walk or were you looking for me?"

"Looking for you." I laughed. "Just wondering if you're still playing hoops."

"You know I am, bro. Every day down at the cage. I play twenty-one most mornings with Badger, Mailman and Fridge . . . when they're taking a break from school." Fly grinned. Clearly his friends took a lot of breaks from Regent Park Junior High.

"So you're still playing with the Running Rebels?"

"Best team in the Park."

"How would you like to play for another team?"

Fly raised an eyebrow. "What other team is that?"

"My team."

"Your team? A bunch of rich, white dudes at a fancy private school?"

"Yeah, Winfield."

Fly shook his head in disbelief. "Why the heck would I do that, bro?"

"Because we need you. Our best player just left town. We need someone who can score twenty points a game. Otherwise we're going to get blown out every time."

"How am I supposed to afford Winfield?" Fly waved an arm. "Just take a look around. We don't exactly have extra cash."

"Coach Bryant said there was one scholarship for a student who couldn't afford to pay."

"Listen to yourself, bro. It's for students. I'm no student."

"But you could be. You're not dumb. You just don't like school. Or at least not Regent Park Junior High."

Fly looked at me long and hard. "I don't know."

"I could help you with your classes." I gave Fly my most convincing smile. It was the smile I'd always give after he'd scored a spectacular bucket in our summer games.

"Hey, Ma!" Fly called. "What do you think of me going to Winfield College?"

"Is that your idea of a joke, Freddie?" She marched out of the kitchen, hands on hips.

"No joke, Ma."

"Then you're going," she said, wagging a finger at him. "And I don't care if you play basketball or not. You have to finish high school."

5 Ready For TAKEOFF

The gym was packed. Everyone in the crowd wanted to see the new guy, the poor kid from the streets of Regent Park. The guy being given a free ride at Winfield College just because he could shoot an orange ball through a hoop. The guy the Wildcats were pinning their entire season on, now that their star player had moved away to the bright lights of New York City.

I stood waiting my turn in the layup line before the game. I knew how the fans felt. Fly's story had swept through the school like wildfire. If I were in the stands I'd want to see Fly Davis, too.

No one had ever seen a player like Fly before. Winfield only played against other small private schools. They never had to battle against street-hardened teams from big public high schools like Regent Park, teams that usually won the city titles.

This was only Fly's second day at Winfield. He'd had barely enough time to find his way to class or to the gym. He hadn't even been to a Wildcats practice and had only been introduced to the team by Coach Bryant a few minutes before in the locker room. There were a lot of sideways glances, especially from Jaxen who was benched to make room for Fly. Everyone was keeping his distance.

Fly stood ahead of me in line. His athletic body looked tired, his eyes sleepy and bored. I didn't know if he even wanted to be there. Maybe the stress of being at a new school and meeting new people was too much.

I should have known better. If there was a crowd watching, Fly was ready to perform. When Kenny passed him the ball he dribbled once, took two long strides then jumped for the basket. No, it was more like he launched himself like a rocket. He flew toward the hoop with the ball grasped in one hand, then slammed it through the iron with a thunderous throw-down. The students went nuts. The game hadn't even begun yet.

Coach Bryant called out the starting line-up. "Brock, Rajeet and Freddie up front. Griffin and Kenny at guard. Let's go!"

The opening tip went to the Brampton Tech Bulls, who quickly broke into our half. The Bulls guard didn't waste any time trying to make things happen. He drove straight for our basket without even looking to make a pass. He took me by surprise. Brock and

Kenny were left flat-footed as well. He scored easily and Kenny inbounded the ball to me. I raced up court scanning for Fly. I wanted to give him the ball for an early hoop to give him confidence. I wanted to show the team, the fans and Coach what he could do.

Fly faked to the outside then cut into the paint just like I had seen him do a hundred times. I delivered a bounce pass like Mailman would have done and Fly grabbed the rock. Spinning toward the basket, he skyed high over the Brampton guard and jammed the ball through the hoop ten feet in the air.

The crowd exploded.

Fly responded by running back to our end like nothing had happened — like this was just normal, like this was going to happen all the time. And it did. After every Brampton bucket we came back to even the score. And almost every time it was Fly who threw down the rock for the two points.

The pace of the game was lightning fast. The ball travelled back and forth across the court, making it more like a tennis match than a basketball game. Sweat poured off bodies. Players sucked big gulps of air while trying to keep up. This was run-and-gun basketball the way it was meant to be played. The way it was played in the cage at Regent Park. The way Fly knew how to play.

The crowd was on its feet. They couldn't stop cheering, couldn't stop being amazed by the power and grace of Fly's moves. Even my teammates were wide-eyed. Sometimes Brock and Raj quit running and just gawked.

As the clock ticked down to halftime the Fly Show continued, with the star popping a couple more buckets. The buzzer echoed through the gym and I headed to the bench to join my teammates huddled around Coach. I glanced at the scoreboard and saw we were up by four. I expected Coach to be happy.

"What's going on out there?" Coach scowled.

Kenny looked confused. "But we're winning, Coach."

"*We're* not winning. *Freddie* is winning. The rest of you guys are just standing around watching him."

"We're getting him the ball," I said.

"You've made some good passes, Griffin. But always to the same guy. Since when are we a one-man team?"

"Since Fly showed up," someone said, under his breath. I turned to see Brock smirking.

Coach grabbed his diagram board and used an erasable marker to draw a play. "In the second half I want to see Rajeet and Brock get the ball." He drew some lines to show how Kenny and I should pass to them. "Everyone got it?"

Everyone nodded. "Got it, Coach."

I looked over at Fly. He was back to looking bored. He cast his eyes aimlessly around the gym.

"Guess we'll have to let some of the other guys touch the ball," I said to him with a laugh.

"Whatever," Fly said. "I'm just here to play my game, bro."

In the second half I did my best to deliver the ball to our two forwards. It wasn't easy. Neither Raj nor Brock had Fly's wheels and they struggled to get open. Just when I thought they were in the clear a Brampton player would slide beside them and steal the pass. Then the Bulls player would hustle down court and hit for a basket. It didn't take long before the game was tied.

I watched Fly out of the corner of my eye. With so much attention being given to Raj and Brock he didn't see the point in getting open. I had quit trying to give him the ball and he had quit trying to get it. Now there was a different look on Fly's face. His eyes had narrowed and his hands were on his hips. He was getting mad.

I shot a glance at the clock. There were less than two minutes left and Brampton was up by three. The tables had turned, all because we weren't willing to give Fly the ball.

Maybe Coach wasn't, but I was.

The next time down the court I faked a pass to Raj and then hit Fly right in the hands. He was so surprised he almost dropped the ball. But he squeezed the rock, turned and hit a fifteen-foot jumper from the top of the key. We were down by one with under a minute in the game.

Run and Gun

Brampton tried to kill the clock by playing keep-away. They passed the ball between their players as Brock and Kenny chased them around. Time was running out. I had to make something happen. Diving in desperation, I picked off a pass and dashed down the court into the Bulls' zone. Fly gave me a nod — a nod I had seen all summer. It meant I was to throw him an alley-oop pass. I tossed the ball above the rim and Fly leaped high. He grabbed the ball in mid-flight, then slammed it hard through the hoop.

The clock ticked off the final seconds. The sound of the buzzer was drowned out by the sound of our cheering fans. The Wildcats had squeezed out a narrow one-point victory.

Fly was mobbed. Raj, Kenny and I all high-fived him. Even Brock pounded fists with him. Only one person in the gym wasn't stoked by our last-minute win. I watched Coach shaking his head as he disappeared into the locker room.

6 STUMPED

It was an easy question. One that any kid in junior high should know. *Who was the first prime minister of Canada?* I glanced around the classroom and saw Brock rolling his eyes. I could tell he thought the question was too lame for him to waste energy raising his hand. Kenny Woo looked happy that he actually knew an answer and his arm shot up.

Miss Fulton stood at the front of the class. She scanned the blue blazers and sweaters hunched over the desks. The teacher looked right past Kenny to the new student sitting behind him. "Freddie, can you tell me who Canada's first prime minister was?"

Fly didn't answer at first. He held Miss Fulton's stare long and hard, slouched in his chair, his long legs stretched into the aisle. After a few seconds he spoke. "No, I can't."

I could hear a few muffled snickers around the room. As usual, Brock was the loudest.

"Do you need a hint?" Miss Fulton smiled. "What's the name of your favourite fast-food restaurant?"

"Burger King," Fly said flatly.

More snickers.

"Hmmm . . ." Miss Fulton sighed. "I was thinking more of the golden arches."

She marched down the aisle and came to a stop beside Fly's size thirteen shoes. "Surely, you can tell me who the father of confederation was?"

Fly tilted his head and gave her a steely glare. "I can't even tell you who my father was, lady."

Miss Fulton raised her eyebrows. I'm sure no one had ever called her that. I could see she was frustrated by Fly's answers, or lack of answers. She turned and went back to the front of the classroom. "Brock, you seem to find this all very funny."

"How could anyone not know it was Sir John A. Macdonald?" mocked Brock.

"Maybe not everyone was taught that in their previous school." Miss Fulton was giving Fly the benefit of the doubt. "Why don't you tell us how you remember his name?"

"It's easy," Brock said, pulling a fat wallet out of his back pocket. "All I have to do is look at the face on this stack of purple tens I carry around with me."

★★★

Fly and I both had free periods at the end of the day. But Winfield didn't let you go home. They thought you'd just slack off, which, of course, was true. The school rule was that you had to study in the library until the final bell.

Fly slumped into the chair beside me. He had loosened his tie and undone the top button of his shirt. The sleeves of his Winfield sweater were rolled up, revealing some tats.

"I hate this tie, this shirt, this sweater. But most of all, I hate being made to look stupid."

"How could you not know that answer?" I asked. "Everyone knows about Sir John A."

"The question is, why do I need to know?"

"But how did you get through school?"

Fly held up his long, ball-gripping hands. "These are what got me through, bro. These led our team to the city finals last year. They scored more than twenty points a game. These hands get teachers to give me marks I probably don't deserve."

"Teachers kept passing you every year just so you could play hoops?"

Fly nodded. "You know the drill, bro. If you don't make the grade, you don't get played."

"Maybe I can help you. We could start with History and learn the different prime ministers. Then move on to English and Math."

"I don't know, man. There are only so many free periods a week. And we have practice most days after school."

"I could come over to your place. We could study at night and on Saturday and Sunday —"

Fly held up his hands again. "Slow down, bro. I've got things to do at night and on the weekends."

"Like what?"

"Like working. My mom's job doesn't bring in enough. And now that I have to walk around in these fancy blue and grey threads, we need more cash every month."

"You work most nights?"

"You know it." Fly chuckled. "I'm the best damn grocery bag boy there is."

Hearing about Fly's life made me realize how easy I had it. I didn't have to get a job during the school year. I always had time to do my homework. And I didn't have to visit a brother who was in jail. Fly had to worry about a whole lot more than just school.

Just then Brock came around the corner. He was holding something tightly in his hand. He must have overheard every word we said.

"Hey, Davis," Brock smirked. "I've got something that will help you study and pay for your Winfield uniform."

Fly clenched his fists.

"Get lost, Brock," I said.

"Our chauffeur is waiting for me outside in a car. But I thought I'd drop off a little present before I went." His face broke into a sly smile as he tossed a ten-dollar bill on the table. Sir John A. Macdonald's crumpled face stared back at us.

17 No Fly ZONE

"Let's go, Wildcats!"

Coach Bryant paced in front of the Winfield bench, shouting instructions. He kept repeating what he had told us in the locker room before the game. "Slow it down. Work the ball around. Find the open man. Wait for a good shot." Same old, same old.

We had managed to keep the score close. In the third quarter we trailed the Richmond Hill Rockets by just two points. We still had lots of time to come back and win.

Kenny passed me the ball and I slowly dribbled up court into the Rockets' half. I passed back to Kenny, who passed to Raj, who passed to Brock, who was supposed to pass to Fly for a shot. But Brock had a different plan. He didn't even look for Fly who was wide open under the basket. Instead, he returned the ball to me. Now we were back to square one.

"Nice work!" Coach shouted from the sideline. "Great ball control."

Run and Gun

We might have controlled the ball but we forgot about one thing — shooting and scoring. We were never going to get the tying bucket if we didn't shoot. There was one other problem — playing ball control was b-o-r-i-n-g.

Fly shot me a glance and I could read his mind. *I'm wasting my time out here, bro. If I don't touch the ball soon I'm going to lose it.*

I sent a bounce pass to Brock. He should have flipped the rock to Fly as he cut up the middle. That was the drill in practice. But Brock put the ball on the floor once and then took a long thirty-foot jumper. I knew it was way out of his range. The ball hit the iron and bounced right into the hands of a waiting Rockets player.

The team in the red uniforms came straight at us. Two laser passes found their tall centre open under the hoop, and he laid it up and in for a four-point lead.

I took the inbounds pass from Kenny and started dribbling. I was tired of walking the ball like Coach wanted. His slowpoke strategy was getting us nowhere fast.

I broke into a run and Fly joined me. We were like two wild horses galloping down court. I zigzagged between the Richmond Hill guards, then fired a chest pass to Fly as he broke in from the right side. He grabbed the ball in one big hand and drove the lane. Fly's eyes flamed like a demon hell-bent on only one goal — taking the rock to the hoop. His body uncoiled as he went airborne above the outstretched arms of the Rockets defenders. In mid-flight he shifted the ball from his left to right hand, then smashed the rock home with a jaw-dropping dunk.

The crowd exploded. So did Coach Bryant.

"Timeout Winfield!" called the ref.

I hustled to our bench where Coach Bryant was waiting. His arms were tightly folded across his chest. "What's going on out there? That's not what we talked about. That's not our game plan." He shot dagger-eyes straight at me.

"But we're losing, Coach," I said. "We need points."

"And we got the basket." Kenny nodded. "Did you see that slam?"

"Yeah, I saw it, all right," Coach said. "But I didn't like it. That's not our game. We don't play run-and-gun basketball here at Winfield. We play control ball. That fast-paced showboat crap is better left on the playground." Coach turned his attention to Fly. "Isn't that right, Mr. Davis?"

Fly stood his ground. "That's how I play, Coach. I run and I score. It's pretty simple. You got a problem with that?"

"Yeah, I've got a problem with that," Coach snapped. "And so will you if you don't change the way you play starting right now. Because if you can't . . ."

I winced, knowing what was coming next.

" . . . You can take a seat right now."

Every head turned to look at Fly, waiting for his next move.

Fly walked calmly over to the bench and sat down. "Then I guess I better get comfortable."

"Let's go, Winfield," the ref said. "Game on."

Coach surveyed the other players on the bench. "Jaxen, go in for Davis."

I walked back on the court eyeing the rest of our team — Brock, Kenny, Raj and Jaxen. Tyler was gone and Fly was sitting on the bench. I didn't know how we were going to come back with this crew. What was left of our team wasn't good enough. And that included me.

I was right. Richmond Hill saw that our star player had been pulled. Now they were on the prowl, hungry to keep the lead. Already ahead by two points, the Rockets moved in for the kill. For the whole fourth quarter they put the pressure on. They intercepted our passes, blocked our shots and snatched away rebounds. By the end of the game we were dragging our butts all over the floor. I hung my head as I trudged off the court and glanced at the scoreboard. We had been blown out: Richmond Hill 72, Winfield 48.

18 SHOWDOWN

At first, no one said a word. Most of us sat on the bench, faces strained, lips tight. Coach was out collecting the game sheets from the ref and timekeeper. The room was dead quiet.

Kenny slammed his locker. "That was the worst game we've ever played!"

Raj nodded. "I don't know what happened. We were totally in it for the first half."

"You don't know what happened?" Brock asked, his face tensing. "I'll tell you what happened. We had a guy who was only playing for himself. A guy who didn't care about the team." He shot a menacing look at Fly sitting alone at the other end of the room. His locker was open and I could see his gym bag at the bottom. It was the same bag he had the night of the shootout in the park.

Fly had already figured out that Brock was a troublemaker. Fly sat back and gave him a long, slow stare that said *you better back off.*

"It wasn't Fly's fault," I said. "He was just trying to score and keep us from falling too far behind."

"Yeah," Kenny said. "How are we supposed to win if we don't make some buckets?"

Brock shook his head. "That's not the way Coach wanted it."

"No, it's not," a voice boomed. Coach Bryant strode into the locker room, clutching the scoresheet. "You guys know exactly what the game plan was." His eyes darted around the room. They were narrow with pent-up rage. "We had a plan and everyone listened except for one guy." Coach took a few steps toward Fly and crossed his arms. "You think you're bigger than the team, Davis? You think you know better than the coach? How to run and gun? How to win games all by yourself?"

Coach paused for a few seconds. I thought he was giving Fly a chance to answer back, to defend himself. But Coach was just getting started.

"I give you a chance for an education at the best private school in the city. And what do I get? I let you wear the colours of a proud team with a long tradition of winning. And what do I get? I give you a chance to learn from a coach who knows how basketball is really played."

Coach took a couple more steps toward Fly until he was standing right over him. He looked down at the best athlete to ever put on a Winfield uniform.

Coach locked eyes with Fly one last time. "And what do I get?"

The strain of Fly's clenched jaw spread through his entire body. His tattooed biceps bulged. His big hands balled into tight fists. His thighs tensed, ready to spring. Fly glared up at Coach, his face stone cold.

"I'll tell you what you get, man." Fly leaped from the bench. He loomed over Coach, his dark eyes filled with rage.

Coach raised his hands and took a step back. His boiling anger had turned to chilling fear. Blood drained from his face. "Take it easy, Davis."

"This is what you get!" Fly waved his clenched fist just inches from Coach's shocked face. "This is what you get for dissing me. For bringing the other players down. For bringing the greatest sport in the world to its knees."

I had to do something. Fly was out of control. Anything could happen next.

I had gotten Fly into this mess. I had to get him out. I inched my way toward him — past Kenny, past Jaxen, past Brock. Their eyes were as wide open as their mouths. "Fly, what do you want from Coach?" I asked, trying to remain calm.

"I want him to respect me," Fly said. "And I want him to respect the game."

"What do you think, Coach?" I asked. "Is Fly one of the best high school players you've ever seen?"

Coach stared at the fist in his face as he spoke. "He's probably the best player I've ever seen. The best player I've ever coached — even better than Tyler."

"You know it." Fly narrowed his eyes as he nodded.

Coach cast his eyes around the room at Raj, Kenny, Brock, Jaxen. "But you can't just come here and change the way we do things here. We play as a team."

Fly started to shake his head at Coach. I locked eyes with my friend and spoke slowly. "If you back away now everything will be okay. Isn't that right, Coach?"

"Okay."

"What do you say, Fly?"

Fly turned and stared at me. It was just like the first time he laid eyes on me in Regent Park, when he wondered whether he could trust a kid like me.

Finally, Fly took a step back and lowered his clenched fist. "He's not worth it, bro. He'll never learn."

I took a deep breath to try to still the jackhammer pounding in my chest. Then I walked Fly to the other end of the locker room.

19 Slow and STEADY

"I could have been killed," Brock said. His voice was still shaky from the standoff in the locker room the day before. "All those Regent Park guys are in gangs and carry guns." He sat at a long table in the cafeteria with the other starters. A plate full of lasagne waited to be scarfed down in front of him.

Raj nodded. "We all could have been beaten up — or shot."

"Gunned down in our own school." Kenny formed a pistol with his thumb and finger, then pretended to shoot Jaxen, Raj and Brock.

"And you know whose fault it all was?" Brock glanced around the table.

Kenny's brow furrowed with confusion. "Fly's, of course."

"Guess again." Brock narrowed his eyes at me.

Three heads turned in my direction.

"Yeah . . . Griffin's," Brock said. "He's the one who knew Fly. The one who played with him last summer. The one who brought him to Coach. I knew we should have stuck with the team we had. Guys like Fly are nothing but trouble. And that scholarship never brought us anyone good." Brock glared at me again. "They aren't like us. They aren't real Winfielders."

I knew that threatening Coach Bryant in the locker room was a dumb thing for Fly to do. But I didn't want to believe Fly would really have punched Coach. He wasn't a bad guy. He just lived a whole different life from us.

"I don't think Fly was really going to hurt anyone," I said. "I think he was just bluffing to get Coach's attention."

"Yeah, well, he got it all right." Brock nodded smugly. "But Winfield will kick him out. He won't be missed."

Then Kenny said what was on everyone's mind. "The team's going to miss his twenty points a game, though."

***

The stands were starting to fill before the next game against the Thornhill Hawks. Winfield students in their white shirts, blue sweaters and grey pants were streaming into the bleachers. A busload of Hawks fans in green blazers were finding their seats. There had been a lot of chatter in the halls and between classes about how well we'd do now that Fly was gone. Everyone wanted to see if the Wildcats could win without their gun-slinging, outlaw star. Most didn't think we had a chance. I didn't want to admit it, but I didn't think we did either.

Coach Bryant stood in front of the bench. He gave his last-minute instructions before the opening tip. "This is a big game for us — a real turning point." He scanned every face on the team to make sure we were paying attention. "This will tell us how we'll do for the rest of the year. The private school league has a short season. We have to make the most of every game if we want to make the playoffs. But we can do it. We're a better team now that Freddie Davis is gone."

Kenny raised an eyebrow. "You're sure we're better without Fly, Coach?"

"Damn sure, son." Coach held Kenny's gaze. "We don't need a show-off who's just out for himself. We need a team that plays together. We don't need to sprint up and down the court. We need to play an even-paced control game. And we don't need a guy who doesn't listen. We need a group of players who will follow my orders. Just you wait and see. I bet that by halftime we'll be way ahead of Thornhill."

"And what if we're not?" Kenny asked.

Coach looked confused, like he had never considered losing. "We'll cross that bridge when we come to it. But that's not going to happen. Now let's get out there and play our game. Wildcats on three."

I put my hand in the middle of the circle formed by the other starters — Brock, Raj, Kenny and Jaxen, who was back in the line-up for Fly.

"One . . . two . . . three . . . Wildcats!"

Raj took his position at centre court and crouched low. The ref tossed the ball up. Raj leaped as high as he could, but the Hawks centre was too big, too strong. He grabbed the rock with both of his huge hands. It was game on.

The Hawks passed the ball around the three-point arc before feeding it inside to a cutting forward. He kissed it off the backboard for the first basket.

It's just two points, I thought. *It's too early to worry. We're still in it.*

Kenny walked the ball up court slowly, just like Coach wanted. No running. No gunning. He sent a bounce pass to me. I made a few dribbles before relaying a pass to Raj. There was nothing tricky about what we were doing. Everyone on the floor and everyone in the stands could see our game plan. We were making obvious passes and keeping to the outside a long way from the hoop.

"Way to go, Wildcats," Coach cheered from the bench. "Pass it around!"

I could almost hear the Hawks smacking their lips, like thieves waiting for their chance to make a steal. Raj was a smart player. He was always getting the highest marks in our Math and Science classes. He knew there was no way we were going to score from so far away. We had to get the ball inside.

Raj was waiting to pass to Jaxen standing at the edge of the key. There was only one problem — so were the Hawks. Just as the ball left Raj's hands a Hawks guard darted in front of Jaxen and snatched it away. The guard raced down court and laid the ball into our hoop. It was probably the easiest basket of his life.

We were already four points down. Now I was worried. But Coach didn't seem to be.

"No problem, Wildcats!" he called, clapping his hands on the sideline. "We'll get it back!"

We tried our best for the rest of the half, following Coach Bryant's old-school strategy of dribbling, passing and shooting at a snail's pace. The strategy we had before Fly joined the team. The Hawks played the exact opposite. They were running all over the court. They forced us to make bad passes and rushed shots on defence while turning steals into fast breaks on offence. I had never seen so many smiles on a team we were playing against. Just like a McDonald's commercial, they were lovin' it.

When the ref blew his whistle to end the first half, the scoreboard told the story. Despite Coach's promise of being in the lead, we were trailing by a dozen points.

In the locker room, Kenny slumped on the bench. He took a swig from his water bottle and glanced up at

Coach. "So what do we do now?"

Coach crossed his arms. "We stay the course. Fight our way through it. Claw our way back two points at a time."

I saw Brock shake his head. Now that surprised me. Normally, Brock agreed with everything Coach said. But even he wasn't buying what Coach was selling today. "If you say so, Coach, but . . ."

Coach narrowed his eyes. "But what, Brock? You have a problem with my game plan? A plan that's worked for my teams for twenty years?"

Brock's eyes fell to the floor. "No, sir."

Kenny had more nerve. "It's just that you said —"

"Said what, Kenny?"

"That if we were losing at half we'd change it up, try something new."

"We don't have the players to try something new. We don't have the speed or talent. And even if we did, we haven't practised that way. No one here knows how to play a fast-break game. The only guy who did was expelled a couple days ago."

"We'd like to try, Coach," I heard a voice say. The voice was mine.

I almost couldn't believe that the words came out of my mouth. It wasn't like me to question Coach Bryant. But I was sick of losing — losing this game, losing my friend Fly and losing the way I knew hoops could be played.

Slow and Steady

Brock and Kenny stared bug-eyed at Coach, wondering what he would say. Coach shifted his arms from across his chest to his hips. "You think you're so smart, Finch? You think you know this game better than me? You think you can run with a team like Thornhill?"

"I don't know, Coach. All I know is that we can't beat them the way we're playing. All we can do is try."

20 New Game PLAN

What had my big mouth done? How were we going to win this game? We weren't the same team without Fly. He was the only reason we had won the last game, right? Fly was the only reason the Running Rebels had won almost every game this summer. Well, Fly, Chopper, Badger, Mailman and Fridge. I had nothing to do with it, did I?

Kenny inbounded the ball to me to start the second half. It was time to shift gears. I knew I couldn't walk the ball up court like before, so I took off. And a funny thing happened — the rest of the Wildcats took off as well.

I raced into the Thornhill zone, dribbling left-hand, right-hand, between my legs. The Hawks backed off, which gave me room to find an open man. Instead of loping into the middle, Raj cut sharply through the paint. I hit him with a bounce pass. All in one motion he scooped up the rock, turned to the rim and released a hook shot. The ball floated through the air, then dropped perfectly through the hoop. *Swish!* Raj charged back, pounding fists with me as he flew by.

Suddenly, the smiles on the Hawks faces were gone.

Kenny guarded the Hawks guard step for step as he dribbled into our zone. He was looking to pass. In the first half I hardly worked up a sweat. Now I was pumped, focused, muscles ready to explode. I thought his first move would be a toss to his teammate in the corner, just like it had been all game long. I was ready. I jumped high to pick it off. Racing up court, I spotted Jaxen running ahead of me. Just like Mailman, I delivered the ball to him at the top of the key. Jaxen grabbed the rock and did his best Fly impersonation, leaping high over a Hawks defender and popping a short jumper that found nothing but the bottom of the net. Another bucket. We were clawing our way back, like Coach had said. We just weren't doing it the slow way Coach had said we would.

I could feel the momentum of the game start to swing. We weren't the same team as in the first half. We weren't following a strict plan from an old playbook. We were cutting loose, playing a style buried inside each of us. We didn't know it, but we had learned something in just those two games Fly had played with us.

Raj was going head to head with the Hawks monster centre, but he wasn't getting pushed around any more. Jaxen was darting left and right, hitting jumpers every time he got his hands on the ball. Kenny was on a tear, dropping three-point bombs from beyond the arc. Even Brock had quit complaining and was hustling all over the court, diving for loose balls.

I had learned something, too. I wasn't the lead-footed, no-talent player Coach said I was. I did know how to play a fast-break game. I could dribble like Badger, pass like Mailman, steal like Chopper. I was a Running Rebel. I had learned how to run and gun with the best team in Regent Park. And now, even without Fly, the Wildcats were running and gunning, too.

With less than a minute left on the clock, the game was tied. I heard Coach shout on the sideline. "Timeout!"

I expected an angry earful. But that's not what we got.

"You guys are proving me wrong," Coach said. He shook his head and smiled. "You weren't the problem with our game, I was. We can play run and gun. I just didn't know how to coach that way." Coach gave me a nod. "Now let's get back out there and keep running."

We sprinted back onto the court. Adrenalin shot through every muscle in our bodies.

Five Hawks players came straight at us, looking for the go-ahead basket. As I watched a twenty-foot jump shot sail toward our basket as if in slow-motion, I prayed that somehow it would miss. The ball hit the iron and bounced off, flying crazily through the air. The giant Hawks centre reached high to grab the rebound, but Raj skyed even higher and muscled the ball away. We had a chance.

Raj flipped me the ball and I rushed into Hawks territory. Brock and Jaxen ran with me like a couple of racing horses. The clock was down to ten seconds. I stopped short and made like I was going to shoot. The Hawks bought the fake and rushed toward me, arms raised high to try to block my last-second shot. But I didn't shoot. Instead, I zipped the ball to Brock who had been left standing alone under the basket. He cushioned the ball off the backboard for the winning two points.

At first, we were in shock. Raj and Jaxen looked at me in disbelief. Brock and Kenny stared slack-jawed at the scoreboard: Winfield 71, Thornhill 70. Finally, it all sank in. As we charged off the court, the crowd was on its feet chanting, "Wildcats win! Wildcats win! Wildcats win!"

21 Cage MATCH

It had been a roller-coaster year. We had started with high hopes and a bunch of returning players. Then Tyler had announced he was leaving and we slid to the bottom. I had thought bringing Fly onto the team was just the boost we needed, but that experiment crashed and burned after only two games. But maybe it was all for the best. In the last few games of the season we realized we didn't have to depend on Fly to win. We could run and shoot and score ourselves. And I felt good knowing I had a hand in our string of late-season victories. That what I learned playing with the Running Rebels had rubbed off on Raj, Jaxen, Brock and Kenny, too. We had all stepped up our game.

"We're going up against the best private school in the city, maybe the country."

The practice was over but the sweat was still dripping as we formed a circle around Coach at centre court. He looked gruff, not like the head of a team that had won the last two games of the season and the league semi-final.

Cage Match

Coach held up his hands to get our attention. "The Lakeview Lakers have won the championship two out of the last three years. They're big, they're strong, they're fast — a real powerhouse." He paused to let the warning sink in. "We made some big changes to our game the last few weeks and we've come away with three victories in a row."

"You know it!" Kenny called out. "Go Wildcats!"

Coach narrowed his eyes at Kenny and went on. "Now we've made it to the final. But let me make one thing clear — we're in tough. We've never faced a team like the Lakers before. Or a player like Dante Green before. It's going to be hard to prepare for them."

I had heard about Lakeview. They had a reputation for attracting all-star talent like Dante. They were like a magnet for players who wanted to win and be scouted by big schools for scholarships.

"If only there was a team we could practise against to get ready," Raj said. "A team that was a lot better than we are." I could see the wheels turning in his head. Raj was trying to solve the problem like it was a question on a math test.

Raj may not have had the answer, but I did. After school I made the long walk to Regent Park and waited outside the cage. Even though it was late fall, there was still a handful of players shooting hoops inside the fence. The air was chilled, the temperature a few degrees above freezing. All in all, not bad if you lived to play hoops every day and had no indoor court to play on.

Chopper and Badger were playing a game of H-O-R-S-E against each other. Chopper had just sunk a long jumper from the top of the key and now it was Badger's turn to match him. They had dressed for the cool day in sweat pants, hoodies and high tops.

At five o'clock I saw my contact winding through the park toward me. He looked the same as when I had last seen him — tall, lean, wiry, strong. The only difference was that this time he didn't look angry.

"I wasn't sure you'd show," I said, reaching out my fist.

"I wasn't sure I would either." Fly pounded my fist with his own. "But I thought about it after you called. And here I am. I owe you that much."

I met Fly's gaze. "You let me down, man."

"I know, bro, and I'm sorry." Fly gave his head half a shake. "I let my mom down, too. Now she hardly lets me out of the house. She was some kind of mad at me for getting booted out of school."

"Do you blame her?"

"No, threatening to beat up another coach was a dumb thing to do. I've got to get better at controlling myself. I was just so mad at how he was making us play."

"You wouldn't be now," I said. "We're running and gunning."

Fly let out a thin laugh. "Guess I showed you guys a thing or two while I was there."

"Yeah, you did. And that's why I'm here. I'm hoping the Running Rebels will practise against us."

Fly raised an eyebrow. "Why?"

"We need to play a team that's a lot better than we are so we won't get blown out in the championship."

Fly shook his head. "I can't do that, bro. I can't go back to your gym. Headmaster Hutton made it clear that I can't go anywhere near Winfield. Plus, there's no way Coach would allow it. And I don't blame him."

"You're right about Coach," I said. "He was pretty shaken up by the whole deal."

Fly nodded. "There's no way the Running Rebels can play against you guys on your turf."

***

"Tell me again why we're out here freezing our butts off on a Saturday morning?" Kenny hugged himself trying to keep warm.

"Quit being such a wimp," I said. A white cloud shot from my mouth with the words. "The sun's out and you can hardly see your breath."

Raj pulled a toque down over his ears. "Let's get this practice going before I get frostbite." He joined the other Wildcats walking into the cage, all wearing their new blue Winfield sweats.

Brock watched the game already being played on the court. "Those guys don't look so tough to me, Griffin. I thought you said they were good."

"They aren't the Running Rebels." I laughed. "They're just a bunch of young kids from the neighbourhood."

Suddenly the metal door to the cage clanged behind us. In walked Fly and his teammates — five of the meanest, most ripped hoop players you could imagine. Chopper, Badger, Mailman and Fridge all had their scowling game faces on. There was nothing matching about their uniforms — torn and ripped hoodies of different colours, stained grey and black sweat pants. They all looked ready to play and take no prisoners.

"Yikes," Brock said, under his breath.

Kenny and Jaxen took a step back as Fly came toward them.

"Don't worry, bros." Fly winked. "I'm not going to punch anyone."

The two Wildcats laughed nervously.

"I hear you guys want to step up your game?" Fly bounced the ball once on the hard asphalt. "Want to learn how to play real run and gun so you can take on Lakeview."

"That's why we're here." I turned to my Winfield teammates. "And remember, guys, Coach can never find out."

Cage Match

Fly palmed the ball in one of his big hands. "Lakeview's a good private school squad, but nothing compared to a team from Regent Park Junior High. We played an exhibition game against them last year."

"How'd you do?" Brock asked. It was clear he doubted that anyone had a chance of beating the Lakers.

"It was close until the game started," Fly said with a straight face. "Then we crushed them by forty."

I could see Brock's eyes pop wide. He wasn't alone. Jaxen, Raj and Kenny all looked as nervous as if they were about to play a bunch of tattooed inmates at a prison. But I knew playing the Running Rebels would be the best chance we had to get ready for the Lakers. Our only chance.

"Let's do this," I said, clapping my hands together. "Let's get schooled in how to really run and gun."

Fly smacked the ball with his hand. "Time for some learning, bros."

22 CLANK

A week later, the Wildcats were in the final game against the Lakers, and there was only one way to win. We had to play the game of our lives.

It wasn't going to be easy. We were going into enemy territory, as the game was being held in Lakeview's gym. Their fans had been in the stands long before game time, cheering their approval every time a Laker sank a shot during warm-up. There was a busload of Winfield supporters, but the Lakeview army was drowning them out.

Our only chance for victory was to play every second as hard as we could from start to finish. No mistakes. No regrets. There was no tomorrow. We had to leave everything out there on the floor.

After the opening tip, we flew into action. We ran up and down the court as fast as we could, always looking for an open man on offence and hustling back on D. And we were gunning every chance we got. Brock, Jaxen and Raj were taking short jumpers from

Clank

inside the key, while Kenny and I were launching long bombs from three-point land. We were doing everything we had learned in our practice game against the Running Rebels. But for some reason we were coming up empty against the Lakers.

It didn't make sense. Lakeview was a good team, maybe a great team. But they weren't the Running Rebels. They could jump, but not sky as high as Fly. They could defend, but not like the sweeping arms of Chopper. And they could pass, but not like Mailman could deliver a ball right to your fingertips.

We struggled right from the first minute. Our passes were being picked off. Our shots were either air balls or clanking off the rim and bouncing harmlessly away. The more we missed, the more tense we got. After a while we were just a giant bundle of nerves.

For every basket we managed to score the gold Laker uniforms knocked down one or two more. Led by their smooth-shooting point guard Dante Green, they had built a commanding 36–24 lead when the buzzer to end the first half was only seconds away. It was like our run-and-gun game plan had no ammo. We were shooting blanks.

Trudging off the court, my arms and legs felt dead tired — as if we had played a whole game. The locker room was quiet as a morgue. Jaxen and Raj slumped on the bench and stared at the floor. Kenny and Brock gazed at the ceiling. No one made eye contact. No one wanted to admit how bad we were playing. I was just thankful Fly wasn't here to see us stink up the joint.

"The game's not over, guys!" Coach Bryant said. He was trying his best to pump us up. "We've got the entire second half to make a comeback. Let's get out there and show Lakeview who they're up against. Bring it in, everyone — Wildcats on three!"

We gave a half-hearted cheer. But we knew the writing was on the wall, and on the scoreboard. We were down by twelve points and it could get worse. The refs whistled us back onto the floor. Halftime was over.

Coming out of the locker room, I kept my head down and tried not to let the deafening roar of the Lakeview crowd get to me. "Yo, TP!"

Did I hear that right? *Is someone calling me TP?* I wondered. *Can't be. This is a Lakeview crowd. Besides, the only person who calls me TP is Fly. And he's back home in Regent Park.*

"You can do it, Griffin!"

Now I'm really imagining things. That sounds like a girl's voice.

I glanced up. Bounding down the stairs from seats in the fourth row were Fly and Serena. I must have looked surprised.

"You seem shocked to see us, bro," called Fly.

"I didn't know you and Serena knew each other," I said as they reached me.

"We see each other at school all the time," Fly said.

Clank

My eyebrows jumped. "You're back at Regent Park Junior High?"

Fly nodded. "You showed me the way, bro. I told myself, if TP can do it, so can I."

Serena's dark eyes lit up. "And we both wanted to see your game, Griffin."

"Yeah, we didn't want to let you down." Fly pulled his flat lid low to hide his face.

"I'm the one letting you down," I said, shaking my head. "We sucked in the first half." Fly locked eyes with me. "You're trying too hard, bro. You all are. Instead of playing run and gun, you should be playing run and *fun*."

"What are you talking about?" I clenched my jaw. "This is serious, man."

Fly shook his head. "Serious is being shot at in the park, bro. This is hoops, the greatest game in the world."

Serena smiled brightly. "You can't score if you're not loose, not having a good time. You've got to chill, Griffin, like it's just another night working at Manny's."

I smiled back at Serena. I tried to hide how happy I was to see her again.

"There's lots of time to come back, TP." Fly grinned. "Two points at a time." Fly took a quick glance toward the bench to make sure Coach hadn't seen him, then disappeared back into the crowd with Serena.

23 Run and FUN

My Wildcat teammates were already warming up when I joined them on the floor for the second half. One look told me exactly how they felt — bummed. Despite Coach's pep talk, the team felt like there was no way we could win. That it was too big a mountain to climb.

I waved them in for a huddle. "We can do this," I said confidently.

"Says you and what NBA pro?" Brock asked. "Is LeBron watching?"

"No, but Fly is."

"Fly is here?" Kenny blurted out, his eyes darting into the crowd.

"Does Coach know?" Jaxen asked worriedly.

"No," I said. "And he's not going to."

"What did Fly say?" Raj asked.

"He says we have to loosen up, enjoy the game."

Brock glanced up at the one-sided scoreboard. "We might as well give it a try. We've got nothing to lose."

Run and Fun

I nodded. "So let's play some run and fun."

The first time I touched the ball I pretended that I was back playing at Regent Park. Like it was a hot summer day, without a care in the world. The ball zipped between my legs as I dribbled smoothly into the Lakers' zone. I spotted Jaxen deep in the corner and fired him a behind-the-back pass, something I would normally never do in a game.

Coach threw up his hands on the sideline. "What kind of pass was that, Finch?"

Jaxen grabbed the ball. He quickly put up a long jumper that arced through the air before dropping through the twine. It was a perfect shot and good for three points. We were on the move. Now we were nine points down, instead of twelve.

Lakeview raced back against us trying to match our speed. Their quick passes criss-crossed the floor, too fast even for them. Their next pass flew out of the hands of a surprised Lakers player and right into Kenny's. He wasted no time throwing a long pass to Raj who had bolted down court as soon as he had seen the interception. Raj caught the pass over his shoulder, took two long steps and laid the ball softly against the backboard for two more points. Down by seven.

"Full-court press!" Coach shouted.

Every Wildcat sprinted to the Lakers' end of the court and blanketed every guy in a gold uniform. Dante had the ball out of bounds and his eyes darted left and right searching for a teammate to pass to. But everyone was covered. He forced a bad throw and Kenny picked it off. In a flash, Kenny spotted Brock driving up the lane and hit him with a bounce pass. Brock scooped up the rock and went airborne, releasing a finger-roll that flipped over the edge of the rim and fell gently through the hoop. We were trailing by only five.

The game seesawed back and forth. Lakeview would knock down a shot and Winfield would answer right back. We were playing loose, running every time we touched the ball and gunning for the hoop every chance we got. Everyone was scoring. Brock, Jaxen and Raj were hitting from up front. Kenny and I were draining buckets from our guard positions.

The crowd was digging every second of the frenzied action. They were standing and cheering more than they were sitting and clapping. I was pumped, knowing that Fly and Serena were up there cheering along with them.

As the clock ticked down in the fourth quarter I shot a glance at the scoreboard. The good news — we had cut the Lakeview lead to only a single point. The bad news — there were only twenty seconds left to play.

I had the ball deep in our zone. We had to race the full length of the court and somehow find a way to score. The Lakers would be ready for anything, but I had an idea for a play they hadn't seen all afternoon. It was a play I had only ever seen Fly pull off. I eyed Raj and mouthed the words, "Alley-oop." Raj nodded and took off for the Lakers' basket.

Raj was our tallest player. If anyone could get above the rim like Fly, it was him. I dribbled across centre court and into Lakeview territory with a gold shirt hanging all over me. I shook him off with a quick cross-over dribble and raced for the top of the key. I saw Raj driving hard to the basket just like he was supposed to.

The Lakers looked confused, wondering what Raj was doing because he didn't have the ball. When they finally figured it out, it was too late. Raj leaped as high as he could, higher than he had all year. Just for a moment I thought I was watching Fly soaring above the rim. That's when I hit him. I tossed the ball so that it reached Raj's outstretched hands at the peak of his jump, straight above the iron. Raj grabbed the rock with both hands and smashed it through the hoop, his face tight with determination.

We were up by one. The buzzer blasted. Game over!

It was a mob scene. Brock, Jaxen, Kenny and I jumped on Raj after his incredible alley-oop basket. The rest of the Wildcats exploded off the bench and piled on, collapsing in a tangled mess of bodies on the gym floor. Coach Bryant dashed onto the court with an ear-to-ear grin, high-fiving every player he saw.

Run and Gun

The Lakeview crowd sat in stunned silence while our Winfield fans were on their feet filling the gym with thunderous cheers.

WIN-FIELD! WIN-FIELD! WIN-FIELD!

After shaking hands with the Lakers, I headed toward the locker room. But I stopped to scan the crowd, hoping two fans were still there. I wanted to thank them for helping me get this far. For making me a better player. For believing in me.

I didn't have to look far. Fly and Serena were standing on the sideline with big smiles on their faces.

"You did it, TP!" they shouted together.

"No, *we* did it!" I beamed. "We couldn't have won without playing run and fun."

Kenny bounded over. "Anybody hungry?"

"A bunch of us are going to Manny's for pizza," Raj said. "Even Brock."

I watched Brock walk up to Fly, not sure what he would do or say. But he quickly reached out for a fist bump. "You should come with us, man."

Fly nodded. "Let's go."

Kenny, Raj and Brock raced to the locker room with the other Wildcats. I stayed for just a bit longer. My friends walked me to the gym door, Fly on one side of me, Serena squeezing my hand on the other.